The Hope of Christmas

An Anthology

By Bud Hanks

Published by Coyote Hill Press, Camano Island, Washington

Layout & Design by Robin S. Hanks

Second Edition, 2020

Printed in the United States

ISBN: 978-0-9912641-9-3 All rights reserved.

Cover: *Christmas Eve.* [No Date Recorded on Shelflist Card] Photograph. Retrieved from the Library of Congress, <www.loc.gov/ item/2004669669/>

Dedicated to:

Northwest Arkansas Writer's Workshop,
& to my best friend, my wife, Jan Hanks.

.

Table of Contents

Preface

Can compassion and forgiveness deliver us from our human frailties? The stories in this book deal with those complex shrouded memories, in the corners of our minds, stopping at a wishing well, but not sure what will be brought to the surface except a bucket with a hole in it.

Yet, that's why we love Christmas, because even an old bucket with a hole in the bottom can once again hold new life, new hopes, and new dreams.

-- Bud Hanks

One More Time

Shadows played peek-a-boo with twilight's realm, while pixie snowflakes danced on a white blanket. Harry and Marcella Thomas stood, admiring nature's beauty, in the open front doorway of the five-gabled, three-story, country house—loaned to them for their family reunion and fiftieth wedding anniversary.

He adjusted the heavy shawl over her shoulders and back of her neck as they shuffled to the front edge of the veranda. A steadfast arm, supportive for forty-nine years, embraced her weakening body from the cold wind; warm lips brushed her cheek, "I hope it all comes together for us this one time," he said.

"I do too, dear."

"You want to know what I'm really thankful for? Our home, in Branson, is only two hours away. I don't need the challenge of driving in these hills, in snow, anymore than I have to after the ice incident last year."

Her smile told him the incident was best forgotten, then snuggled her head on his chest and squeezed his hand.

The circular drive and hedgerow of evergreens glistened with fresh crystals. The swaying trees bowed to the virgins of winter and started their first courtship of the season.

A puffy flake tiptoed onto his outstretched palm, then vanished before he could bring it close to show her. "The delicate beauty of new melts quickly," he said.

"Except with you, dear," she said. Her smile beamed. "This is such a wonderful Christmas gift Goodwin and Gladys gave us to use—two weeks in their beautiful country home."

"I was shocked when our kids called last summer and asked what we wanted most for our fiftieth Christmas and wedding anniversary this year. I imagined the chagrin on their faces when we told them we wanted to have the whole family together, one more time."

She gave his hand a gentle squeeze. "You've told me all this before."

"I don't seem to remember anymore," he whined. "I don't even remember who owns this property."

Her brow wrinkled. "Goodwin must not have told you Gladys is the only grandchild and inherited the property from her grandparents, the Christmas'. Her Uncle Jack was killed in the war and had never married."

He saw her concerned look. "No, I didn't know that . . . if I did, I forgot. I do know their two kids died here!" he blurted. "Ever since, they like to travel during the Christmas season."

"That's very sad for them. I'm sorry that happened; however, this house couldn't be better for our family reunion."

He struggled to recall, "Don't you remember how much our kids disliked each other growing up? I wasn't sure they would ever speak again, much less visit in the same house. I can understand that Clay didn't want Jane tagging along or bugging him since he was eight years older. But…there was some kind of incident. Do you remember, Mother? I've forgotten."

Her melancholy tone reminded him she didn't really want to remember. "You're referring to the incident that sealed two fates, if only in their eyes. When Jane found Clay's first love letter, took it to school and not only read it to her class but had it printed in the school paper."

"Oh, I had forgotten that, but . . . the relationship between Jane and Laura, with only two years difference, never made sense. I...I could only surmise it was because Laura had severe depression problems since puberty. I was thrilled when, after twenty years, she found a doctor and medication that gave her and her family some inner-peace. The grandkids are a different story. They seem to like each other. E-mail, texting and Facebook definitely helped some relationships."

Not wanting to upset him while he was rambling, she waited. When he finished, she said, "Grandkids are the reasons you have children."

"So true, so true. Right now we need to get you back inside or you'll be chilled to the bone and have to stay in bed the whole time the kids and grandkids are here. We don't want that," he said, shaking his head no.

She held his arm as they ambled through the snow to the open doorway, pausing long enough at the mistletoe-draped threshold for a kiss. Inside, the parlor fireplace crackled and popped welcoming them back.

The banner over the mantel said it all: Good and Glad Tidings wish you a Jolly-Holly Christmas.

On his way into the parlor, he had opened and perused a letter found on the foyer table. "Goodwin left instructions on how to operate all the equipment and appliances. You know I'm mechanically challenged, "he said then snickered. *What she doesn't know won't hurt her.*

"I know, dear. Retired university professors are thinkers, not doers. Now you know why I don't ask you to fix anything. I can't afford to have you fingerless."

"I was relieved when Goodwin told me not to worry about bringing decorations and displays. Everything we need is easy assembly and stored in the carriage house." He sucked in a quick gulp of air. "Mother, I really think the biggest thrill of all will be on New Year's Eve when Santa rides by in his sleigh pulled by six caribou."

"Caribou!"

"Beats a bag man on a dogsled," he quipped. He saw her smile at his quick comeback. "I thought I mentioned that Goodwin's neighbor raises caribou and trained them to pull a sleigh. He always comes on Christmas Eve for the neighbors, but this year he's coming on our special Christmas—New Years Eve."

"No, Professor," she said. Her smile beamed. "You never mentioned that."

"I must've been trying to surprise everyone, including you. I hope the recent weather report is correct about the snow days. It would be great to get six to eight inches of snow Christmas Eve, with a big snowstorm due on New Years Eve night. It would certainly help the outside activities. Why don't you sit by the fire, Mother? Can I get you some tea? We can list the Christmas displays and assign family groups—"

She raised her right hand to stop him. The cough and chills started even though she had on a sweater and shawl. "Tea, please," she coughed out. *It was too bad it came back, she mused. The doctors told her she could lick it, but she knew it was in her lungs.*

"Mother, why did I come in the kitchen?"

"To get some tea for us. I think Gladys said the bags are above the stove."

"I found it. Wish I didn't—"

"Can't you find yourself?" she said, then cackled and coughed. "I would be happy to know who you really are."

"Oh, you're funny. At least I get to meet new friends every day."

"Yes, but they're the same people in the park."

"They look different to me."

"That's because they change clothes," she said, before thinking that her silliness might hurt his feelings.

He came in with the tea on a silver service, a glisten of moisture in the corners of his eyes. "As long as I can still know you, feel the touch of your hand in mine and the beat of your heart next to me when we go to bed, I want to live. Without all that—"

Her eyes said *that's enough*. She helped him place the service on the centered teacart—arranged as an end table for the sofa—when he maneuvered to sit down beside her. She took his hands in hers, "Your beautiful sentiment warms me body and soul. You know I'll always be with you, either way."

After pouring the steeped-tea, they sat with their personal thoughts and the sounds-of-silence: breathing, sipping, crackling.

When tea was over, she smiled and said, "Let me help you take the tea service to the kitchen."

The country kitchen was twice the size of modern kitchens. The fieldstone and brick, baking fireplace highlighted the northeast wall. A six-chaired harvest-table nestled by the back wall for children or extra company. The cast-iron stove stood on lion's paws near mudroom door side. Two bay windows, on each side of the marble-countered sink, allowed panoramic views.

She placed the dishes in the sink and said, "Do you still know how to play the piano?"

"Not sure," he said, turned and shuffled to the piano. "I can take a look and see what's there."

Looking in the piano bench, he found sheet music for 'Beautiful Dreamer', the first song he ever played from memory. His stiff fingers struggled through the stanzas.

"That's very good for someone who hasn't played much in the last fifty years. I would like to see you play more."

"I'm really tired tonight. Can we go to bed?"

"I want you to promise to practice tomorrow then you can play for me and the children. You're too talented to let it go to waste."

"Okay. Another Bach, right?"

They held hands and started up the stairs. "I'll practice tomorrow. I may even learn 'White Christmas' and 'Jingle Bells' before the kids get here," he said, helping her the rest of the way up the winding cherry staircase to the only bedroom with a featherbed. He'd made a point of asking Goodwin about one. She loved featherbeds.

The next morning, he rose early and went down to the kitchen to make coffee as he had everyday since retiring. He knew she'd sleep in and awaken around seven-thirty.

He turned on the Weather Channel and walked to the kitchen window. It appeared the weatherman was right, only a couple of inches of snow had fallen all night.

However, the drifts made some areas of the yard appear a couple feet deep. Goodwin had said not to worry about being snowed in. The root cellar and basement had enough emergency provisions to last four weeks.

The phone rang. *I hope they aren't looking for Goodwin.*

It was Jane—their baby.

"Can we come out right after our Christmas party, Dad? Would it be a bother?"

"No bother, Jane. Everything is ready. We would love to have y'all come early and be with us. Any time you can allot will please Mother."

"And you, Dad?"

"Yes, Jane. I'd appreciate it also. You and the family can help me get started with the special Christmas decorations the Tidings left for us."

"The Tidings?"

"Yes. That's an unusual name, I know. But I'm here to tell you that they're very special. Just wait till you see this great house they let us use."

"Is Clay and his fifth family coming?"

"The last time I checked, he was still a member of our family. You did all agree. Let's keep it civil for Mother."

"You're right, Dad. But then you're always right. Right?"

"Come anytime," he concluded with all the enthusiasm he could muster.

The girl is just like her father: blunt to a fault.

The weekly weather planner came on, and the floorboards upstairs said she was up early. A few minutes later she came down the stairs.

"I'm in here, Mother. Why are you up early?"

"To listen to you practice the piano like you said you would."

"That was a joke last night."

"Joke yourself to the piano while I make breakfast."

"Are you sure I can't help in the kitchen? Are you weak? You remember when you had the last spell and dropped the frying pan?"

"The only thing dropping will be the pan that bonks you, if you don't practice."

"You're just like my piano teacher, Mrs. Buck," he groused on the way to the piano. *She never accepted excuses until the task was completed. Then you could complain all you wanted, but the lesson was over.*

The sheet music for 'Beautiful Dreamer' was still on the stand. He tried singing along as he pecked out the keys. Without thinking about what he was looking at, the notes came back to his memory. Soon, he could play the melody and it didn't sound bad, even if he did say so.

"That was great; however, it didn't sound like 'White

Christmas' or 'Jingle Bells.' Why don't you come eat, and then practice the Christmas songs?"

He sat at the harvest table and watched cardinals at the feeders. His eye caught the expanse of snow stretching to the back of a large hill where the toboggan and inner tube races would take place. Anticipating the speed of his new toboggan, he had a fleeting thought: *The grandkids will be surprised.*

She gave him a noogie. "You're daydreaming. Your food's getting cold."

"Did you see the cardinals?"

"Yes, but I can't figure out why the male keeps flying into the window pane."

"Must be territorial, or he's like me trying to get his point across. I wouldn't worry about it; males are hardheaded. Good breakfast today."

"It's the same oatmeal and toast I usually make you."

"You say that, but I'll be glad if you didn't put any bran in my oatmeal like you did last week. I wouldn't be able to get away from the house long enough to check the decorations in the carriage house, or do anything around here."

"You are so silly. A little bran doesn't hurt you. It helps."

"Did you forget? I'm the guy who doesn't need a little help; I do just fine on my own. About the sixth time I was in the bathroom that day, I almost decided to redecorate."

"You can work without fear today. No bran."

"Then I better get busy. Can I do anything for you before I go?"

"I still haven't heard 'Jingle Bells' or 'White Christmas.'"

"I really need to check out the displays, Honey."

"There won't be any honey for Mr. Honey Bunny, if you don't play for me."

"Ok! 'Jingle Bells' it is. Hope I can't find any sheet music," his voice trailing.

Opening the bench, 'Jingle Bells' stared back.

After ten stumbling versions, the keys tinkled in time. Almost sounded like he knew what he was doing.

"All right, Mother, I practiced. Can I go out and play now?"

"That was wonderful. The children will be elated. You may go, but no foolishness."

"Is there anything I can do for you now?"

"I'm feeling tired; turn on HGTV, please."

"Sure thing. You take it easy and call me if you need me. Goodwin left some walkie-talkies that work within a mile of each other. I'll leave one with you and take one with me. Just press the red button to talk. To hear me, let go of the button."

"I think I still know how to use walkie-talkies. Get!"

He went to the mudroom, pulled on his muck boots and clumped out through the snow. The carriage house was a good seventy-five yards from the main house. In daylight, the size was even more impressive.

You could put one and a half barns in this building. It'll make a great gift to their church.

The solid oak front doors slid open with no effort—perfectly balanced; the handles placed high to keep small kids out.

Approaching the left side of his truck, parked in the center of the building, he turned on the light switch near the loft ladder. The stalls and shelves had section placards and were filled with ornaments and displays for every major holiday.

He walked the entire ground floor and was startled to find the northwest and southwest corners were oversized and converted with a hydraulic lift with tracks like a roundhouse.

Both lifts had a handrail and control box with a green and red button. He stepped on the lift closest to him, pushed the green button and the platform ascended stopping at the loft.

The major Christmas decorations and four large displays were on railcars. Viewing the work involved, he knew he would have to wait for help. He punched the green button and descended.

He hadn't paid much attention to train tracks, or anything else that tried to enter his tired mind when they drove up to the property yesterday. He later recalled, Goodwin had mentioned there was a small train and track laid out on the property. Toy train—Lionel—had crossed his mind. Goodwin's instructions said each display had a specific site and would be easy to handle.

Mother, on the other hand, had noticed the interior of the house the moment she entered and walked through. She was very impressed with the old world charm, and had told him more than once. Beautiful antiques and three fireplaces were interspersed throughout: The parlor had a Steinway as the focal point. A French-Provincial armoire with a T.V. in it, and Louis Thirteenth sofa and chairs highlighted the rest of the room. A Queen Anne sofa, end chairs, butler cart, and Victorian flowered wallpaper fit perfectly in the library. An Arkansas black walnut dining-room set, which seated twenty, with a solid cherry buffet and serving table, portrayed Early-American.

While reminiscing, the walkie-talkie went off, and he hurriedly dug it out of his jacket—fumbling fingers. "Yes, ma'am, do you need me to come in?"

"No," she said, "I was just checking on you. Do you have on your hat, coat, and gloves?"

He laughed. "Yes, I'm fine. This is some carriage house, and the holiday displays are fantastic. I just rode on a hydraulic lift."

"We're not here for you to play Tarzan or get hurt!"

"I'm being careful. Don't worry about me."

"That's what you said last Christmas, when you got vertigo while up the ladder to put the angel on top of the tree, and looked like a gooney bird flapping its wings when you rode the tree down."

"It was a soft landing."

"Yes, I know. only one broken rib. You don't want me to come out there."

"No, dear. That's the last thing."

"What did you say?"

"I said there's a great swing."

"You can show it to me later. Be careful. Don't ruin Christmas for the kids and grandkids. There's the toboggan race, and you promised every grandchild that you would race with them."

"Yes, ma'am." He saluted her direction. "I won't be long."

The instructions said to locate the steam-operated engine before doing anything else. He shook his head. Why couldn't he remember to follow instructions? Wandering out the back door, he saw a set of faint tracks in the snow leading to a miniature barn. Inside, the little engine that could.

The boiler stoked; the engine chugged slow. Once around the property would give him a better idea where all the displays should be placed. He ducked his head and cleared the low overhang.

The little engine picked up speed and puffed towards the side of the house. The braided cord near his left hand looked interesting. A short tug—the loud and clear blast startled him. His forehead crinkled. The train started away from the house, headed for a clump of trees by the creek. She came out the front door and yelled something. The engine was loud and the cowcatcher was pitching snow like a scraper in a Montana blizzard—no visibility. He slowed the engine, allowing him to see. He looked back but she had gone inside—*bread and water for dinner*.

The sidings and markers were located for each display. Goodwin's map identified the weatherproof electrical plugs. Driving back to the barn, he decided:

The grandkids will love to ride this train.

He shutdown the engine and secured the carriage house. Walking to the main house, he prayed he didn't have any episodes where he couldn't find the instruction letter from Goodwin. He decided to put all instructions on the refrigerator.

When he opened the back door and stepped into the mudroom to take off his boots, the aroma of fresh baked pie encircled him. Climbing the short flight of stairs to the kitchen, he could see two baked pies on the butcher-block island table. "A little early to be baking all that, isn't it?" he said to an empty room.

"Did you have a nice choo-choo ride, Mr. Engineer?" she said, walking up behind him, urging the last of his gray hair to turn white.

"My God!" he screamed and levitated onto his toes. "Where were you? You could have caused me to have a heart attack, sneaking up on a soul like that!"

"I was in the walk-in pantry, right behind you. You'll think heart attack, if you ever drive that train at high speed again. There's a cot in the basement with your name on it. If you want to do something constructive, find a Christmas tree and put it up. Even though the families won't be here for a few more days, it would still be nice to have the spirit of the holidays in the house. And the answer on the pies . . . I had to try out the baking oven-fireplace. It reminded me of my grandmother's home."

He said sheepishly, "I think Goodwin told me they kept a

small tree and some decorations under the stairwell. I'll take a look."

On his way there, he heard the national weather report: chance of light snow again tonight. *Light snow. I was just outside and the sky said: I'm undecided, and I'll tell you what I think later.*

Flicking the switch, the storage area appeared larger than from the outside and contained: old toys, Christmas decorations, and a seven-foot high artificial tree. A door led into the back wall. Inside, a single bulb cast shadow-light down a narrow staircase.

He reminded himself. *If I get caught in the walls of this house and don't get the tree up, I'll be the main course for dinner.*

Maybe a quick peek, his imp said; he started down the staircase. At the bottom step, a metal lever jutted from the door. Moving the lever to the right, the wall panel opened, and he stepped into the basement. The entertainment room looked inviting: a sofa, ottoman, television, and a few storage items. Hearing footsteps on the wooden floor above, he scurried back up.

Undoing the dust cover, he placed the tree near the foyer staircase to be seen on entering the house. The three boxes of decorations and lights were enough to complete the tree. An old box of silver tinsel, found on a shelf, draped each bough like she had done when the kids were growing up.

"The tree is up and decorated. You want to approve it?"

"You know I trust you," the hurried voice from the kitchen rang out. "See if you can find some garlands or wreaths for inside the front windows and door."

"Slave driver," he whispered at the kitchen. The clock chimed three p.m. "There's always tomorrow." No answer motivated him.

One entry garland and one door wreath were located in the two remaining boxes. Retrieving the four-foot stepladder from the stairwell, he hung the mantle mistletoe and a string of garland around the doorway.

"Dinner's on," she called. "You don't want it to get cold. And where's the ornament for the top of the tree?"

Hurrying into the kitchen, he saw a small wall hanging latched to the right and a porthole with a clear view of the parlor and foyer. Sneaky. No wonder she didn't have to come out and check the tree. She was peeking.

"What are we having tonight?"

"Grilled cheese and soup, tomorrow night soup and grilled cheese."

The Christmas Eve meal had always been the same when there was family: baked cinnamon-sugar piecrust to whet your palate, a main course of ham salad sandwiches—actually pieces of ham ground up with bologna. The hamlogna slathered on homemade bread right from the oven. The flavor on his mind's tongue made his mouth water.

A multitude of delights would top off the meal: melt-in-your-mouth apple pie, homemade candies, a rowdy taffy pull, and hand-cranked, vanilla ice cream.

After the kids left the nest, they still had *hamlogna* on Christmas Eve, but not this time. It would have to wait until New Year's Eve.

He lit a candle and turned off the television and kitchen lights. They sat and watched new snowflakes flitter outside—silent memories.

When supper was over, he helped with the dishes as usual. The kitchen cleaned; they retired to the parlor where he built a fire and put on the television for her.

"I've got to get more decorations."

Back in the stairwell storage, he found an old silver star and climbed the staircase to top off the tree.

After turning on the tree lights and checking for missing or burned out bulbs, he went back to the parlor for the evening news.

The phone rang early the next day—Christmas day. It was Jane, and she was crying. "Yes, I'm up as usual. Mother's still in bed." Trying to distract her, he said,

"You should have seen the beautiful snowfalls we've had."

"We're having a little trouble getting away, Dad," she sobbed.

"What's the problem?" he cajoled.

"I had an argument with Uncle Ted at his Christmas party last night. You know how righteously correct he thinks he is. It must run in the family. Dick's two boys said they didn't want to go to his house or come to yours. While we were gone, they took my car—no insurance—on a double date. When they got home, I grounded them and sent them to their Uncle Larry. I didn't want them causing a problem for you and Mom."

"Who isn't full of piss-n-vinegar at seventeen and twenty? I realize the boys don't feel they're part of our family, because they're from Dick's first marriage. But they are. You're right, Jane. There isn't any need to disrupt everyone's Christmas because of bad attitudes. Call if you have trouble with the directions to the house. They're fairly straightforward."

"We should be able to make it tomorrow, Dad. And thanks for listening."

"No problem, you know I don't mind helping out with advice if I can. Tomorrow then."

No sooner had the phone hit the cradle, than Clay called. "Dad, I can book a quick inexpensive flight for Rod and Steve out of Cleveland to Little Rock; however, I won't be able to pick them up. We won't arrive until two days later. My ex is giving me fits."

"Not a problem, Clay. I can pick them up at the airport, and they can help me put up some of the great Christmas displays that are here."

"They'll be in tomorrow morning at ten."

"Tomorrow at ten, I'll be there. Drive careful son, we have a lot of fun things planned."

By the time he got off the phone with Clay, he could smell bacon cooking, and he hadn't even heard her come downstairs.

"Did you get your coffee?" he asked.

"Yes, but it's a bit strong this morning."

"I'm still trying to figure out the exact amount of beans to grind to make a good brew. This isn't our coffee maker."

"I know. Thank you. By the way, has the phone been ringing this morning, or am I imagining it?"

"It's not your imagination. First, Jane called. She had a confrontation with my brother during the Christmas party at his house last night—like old times. Then, after getting back home, she found the boys had taken one of the cars that didn't have insurance and gone out with their girlfriends. She said the boys didn't want to come see us anyway. After the boys got back home, she took the keys and grounded them."

"How will she get away if the boys don't have supervision?"

"They'll be staying with Dick's brother, Larry. Since he's a cop, it should be interesting."

"Any other good news?"

"Clay called. Rod and Steve will fly in tomorrow. I have to pick them up. Clay and the gang won't be in for two more days."

The next morning he was at the airport early, drinking coffee in the lounge. The flight was delayed due to a heavy snowstorm in the Cleveland area. Every five minutes he would walk over to the arrivals monitor and check the flight—glad the light snow last night did not contain ice.

Thirty-two minutes past before the incoming flight was

announced. Meeting the boys at the security gate, he said, "My, how you both have grown. How was the flight?"

"Great, Grandpa!" Steve yelled, picking him up in a bear hug,

His eyes bulged, "Steve! You're killing me!"

Steve dropped him. Rod laughed and said, "Can I help you put your eyes back in, Grandpa?"

"You don't know your own strength, Steve," he said, gasping for air. "I hope when you wrestle, you let your opponents live."

"How about if I just shake your hand, Grandpa?" Rod said.

He grabbed both boys in a group hug and kissed them on the cheek, "Any baggage?"

They both held up small tote bags.

"Packing light? How was the trip?"

Steve's eyes lit-up, "The plane hit some air pockets and dropped a few hundred feet each time. Everyone was screaming, but I thought it was fun."

"And you, Rod?"

"It was scary, but Steve's crazy."

"Aren't we all when we're young?" The two boys nodded in agreement. "Let's get out to the house. Grandma has some treats for y'all, and I've got some Christmas displays you can help with. Don't forget your manners; you're in the South. It's yes, Ma'am and yes, Sir—with a few y'alls thrown in for good measure."

Steve winked at Rod and mocked, "Right on Grandpa, y'all ready?"

* * * *

"Wow!" Steve exclaimed as they turned into the drive. "This place is beautiful."

"Yeah, it's not bad," said Rod. "I wish dad was here."

"He called and said he and the family would be along in a

couple of days, not to worry. Now that y'all are in high school, and your dad has a better job, he's hoping for a better relationship. We're all sorry that it's been so strained. Y'all remember, Grandma and I will always love each of you and be there for you. Let's go say hello to Grandma before she comes out of the house looking for us. Take your bags in with you."

By the time he got in the house, after putting the truck away, the boys were finishing their first batch of warm cookies and milk.

"Any left for me?"

"You know there is," she said, pushing a plate of hot cookies toward him. "Now sit down and I'll get you some milk."

After cookies and milk, he said, "You boys ready to help me set out some displays? Probably help work up an appetite, and it will spruce up the place before everyone gets here."

"Sure," they chimed.

"Let's go out to the carriage house and take a look. You can tell me what you think."

"No, Tarzan," she said. "The boys don't need a bad example."

On the way to the carriage house, Steve said, "What did Grandma mean, no Tarzan?"

"She was referring to what I found in the carriage house. I'll show you the displays and hydraulic lifts."

When the boys saw the displays on the ground floor, they were impressed. "Now I'll show you my Tarzan apparatus. Step on," he said. They rode up.

"Cool!" Steve exclaimed. "This is awesome. It's almost as good as that plane ride. How do you get these displays out of here?"

He followed the instructions, and the boys helped him maneuver one display at a time to the lift.

As the first display was loaded on, he said, "Steve, you take this one down and pull it out to the siding. Rod, you take the second one, and I'll take the third."

After all three displays were put in position for towing, he said, "Ok, boys, let's go to the engine house."

They helped him stoke the boiler. Rod was assigned as oiler and Steve as brakeman. Steve and Rod got on the coal car for the ride around the property.

Grandpa said, "Watch your heads on the way out."

When they cleared the overhang, Rod yelled, "Stop! Grandpa! Steve lost his head."

"The snow will preserve it till we get back," he said. The engine picked up speed; a synapse fired—*cot in the basement*.

Arriving at each display site, he stopped the train and explained how the sites worked, and how the boys should secure each display and light it up. "Any questions?"

None heard, they finished the property tour; backed onto the siding next to the carriage house and hooked up the first display. The *Santa and reindeer* was towed to its designated site. "Steve, why don't you take this one," he said. "The electrical box is under that fake lily pad."

The *Snowman, with top hat and pipe* was pulled to its site. He dropped Rod off and said, "Be sure and release the arm latch so Frosty can wave to everyone driving by the house."

"No problem, Grandpa. Y'all come back now, ya here."

He drove back and hooked up *Hark The Herald Angels Sing* How appropriate to have the angels by the creek near the trees. The singing should be beautiful.

The boys finished and were walking through the snow towards the house. Putting the engine in reverse, he backed to them and said, "Thank you, boys, that will be enough work for the day. Steve, don't forget your head. Must be time for more milk and cookies. Don't ruin dinner. Grandma is making homemade tacos tonight. Y'all can help with supper. I'll tend the engine and secure the carriage house, then I'll be in."

By the time he got in the house, the boys were eating cookies and telling grandma about all the great displays and decorations in the carriage loft. She just winked as he walked past to wash up.

Everyone else slept in the next day, but he was up by six-fifteen making the morning coffee. His sniffer finally agreed: smelled like homebrewed.

The phone startled him. It was Jane.

"We'll be there today around one thirty, Dad."

Jane, Dick, and Patricia Ursa Minor—Pam for short—arrived at one thirty-one, almost as predicted. Why they'd ever named their daughter Ursa Minor, just because they were into Astronomy at the time of conception, was beyond his comprehension. *Better than R2D2, I suppose.*

Rod and Steve were given a room in the basement with their own shower and bathroom. The old Murphy bed would work for them. Jane's family was designated the front room upstairs–one of the smaller bedrooms.

Clay's family needed the biggest. Laura's family would be fine in the small one. If Jim came, he could stay in the basement with Rod and Steve.

After everyone got settled, the house was quiet.

Not feeling like a nap, he went under the staircase and down the narrow stairs with only a creak or two.

Nearing the bottom, he heard Rod and Steve talking, watching television, and munching loudly. Moving the handle, he let out a banshee scream and pushed the panel open. Not knowing that his wife had washed sheets and hung them to dry on the clotheslines, he ran into a sheet and looked like a real evil ghoul coming out of the wall. The boys screamed; cookies and milk flew.

The sofa, where they had been sitting, was knocked over in their mad scramble to escape certain death. They huddled behind it looking for a weapon to use.

Almost strangling himself on the clothesline, he fell over an old washboard and landed on the ottoman. The sheet flew off and the boys quit screaming.

Rod choked on his cookie. Steve applied the Heimlich and yelled, "Grandpa! I think I had a heart attack!"

Everyone in the basement started laughing or coughing, but not those family members upstairs. Dick and Jane should have been on the Olympic sprint team.

They made it from the third floor in record time.

Grandma was at the top of the stairs yelling, "Do I have to come down there? What's going on?"

"We're okay, Mother. We were just having a little fun," Grandpa said.

"A little fun, my ear. It sounds like one of those bad 'B' movies we used to watch, like Killer Tomatoes."

"I'll explain when I come upstairs."

"Why don't you get up here now and greet Clay at the front door, so I can get back to the kitchen? The cookies are burning."

As he started up the stairs, Steve yelled, "Paybacks are hell, Grandpa."

His broad grin energized the moment. "You wouldn't hurt an old man with glasses, would you?"

"As you're so fond of saying," Rod said, "there's more than one way to skin a cat."

Clay and his new family were coming in the front door. *Rod and Steve would be elated that their dad had come early.* "You look in great shape," he said, as he hugged Clay and gave him a kiss.

"Rod and Steve are in the basement, and they can't wait to see you."

"I'll go down as soon as I get the suitcases to the room, Dad. I can't wait to see them; it's been a while. You remember all my other kids?"

"Let's see: Peter, Paul and Mary. No, that's not right. The memory is getting worse I'm afraid—out of sight, out of mind."

Clay gave his dad a queried glance, as he and the three kids started up the staircase with the luggage. "I'll reintroduce them when I come down, Dad. Which room?"

"The big bedroom, third door on the left." His voice drifted to Clay's wife. "Well Sunny, how have you been?"

She forced a smile, "Clay still won't let himself believe you and mom aren't doing well. We talked about having you both come and live with us, or at least stay close enough we could help every day. Problems came up: our son Joseph, the business, then Carol came back home and is going to have a baby. Following your example, we took her in. We knew we were over-committed and couldn't take care of you and mom the way we want. Clay is fit to be tied and stressed."

"Tell him I have a long-term care-plan for Mother and me, and he doesn't have to stress out anymore. I'm sorry I even asked y'all."

"Are you sure? We still have more options to explore."

Giving her a kiss on the cheek, "I'm sure. Don't worry. Why don't you get some rest? You must be frazzled after riding with Clay."

Starting for the stairs, she said, "He's toned down, but I'm still looking for more. I've worn out at least sixteen purses throwing them out of the van as we fly past a station where I can go to the bathroom."

"I heard that," Clay said from the top of the stairs.

"I'm going to the basement to see my boys. Dad, Joseph, Mary, and Peter are unpacking and hanging clothes. Get to know them better. What a great room, Sunny. You'll love it."

Jane walked in from the front veranda and said, "Where's Mom? I thought I'd help out in the kitchen. By the way, Dad, you've got a fantastic view from the front porch."

"Veranda," he said. "Just saying it adds character to a home."

"You win, Dad. Veranda."

"Mother's in the kitchen. Thanks for offering to help. She gets tired and won't rest when there's company."

"Can I help, Mom?" Jane asked, seeing her mother bent over the sink.

"Yes, of course. I always liked to have you kids in the kitchen. That's why y'all are excellent cooks in your own right."

Jane laughed, "That's not what Dad says. He said he taught you everything you know. Says he's actually responsible for all the great cooks in the family."

She laughed until she started to cough. When she got her voice back, she said, "Your father would take credit for inventing the world, if he didn't think God would get jealous."

They both laughed until they cried. Her cough escalated.

"Are you not any better, Mom? Dad seems about the same. Anyway, Dick and I have been racking our brains to come up with a solution for you and Dad. But with the two boys causing so much headache and heartache right now, we just don't know what to do. My new job as Director is going to have longer hours, and Dick just started his own business. There's a nice nursing home not far from us, but I know you and Dad don't want to go there, yet."

"No. Not yet. Your dad is immured mentally in moments of

time. Not to worry though, Dad and I have a long-term care-plan for the future. Let's get supper started."

Everyone was seated at the table when the phone rang. "Bet it's Laura," Clay said.

"Bet it's Bill," Jane said.

"Would you get that, Harry?" Grandma asked.

He answered the phone, cupped the receiver with his hand, and said, "You're both wrong. It's our granddaughter, Hunny. Thanks for calling, Hunny, and letting us know. See you then." He returned to the table. "They'll be here tomorrow, Mother."

"Grandpa, why would anyone name their kids after organic sounding stuff?" Rod asked.

"Why, I think Hunny and Rosemary are pretty names, don't you, Pam?"

"Yes," Pam said. Her made-for-TV smile spoke volumes. "They're beautiful names, just like mine."

"Tomorrow we have some work for everyone, and then inner tube races," Grandpa said.

"When are the toboggan races, Grandpa?" Steve asked.

"When Laura, Bill, and the kids get here. Tonight Grandma and I have a Dictionary contest with prizes…everyone can participate. Did I ever tell you my mother invented something similar to the game back in the 1940's?"

"Yes, Grandpa," they all chorused. "You've told us a thousand times."

Grandma winked at him, but Jane caught a glint of sadness in his eyes.

The next day everyone participated: setting displays, putting up Christmas decorations, and securing a blowup Santa, with toy bag, in the top of the chimney that wasn't going to be used. All you could see from the yard was Santa's boots, part of the toy bag, and his red pants.

One large display from the loft and the large manger scene were left for Laura's family to put up. Everyone agreed the crowning moment would come when Hunny and Rosemary, dressed as angels, would carry the baby Jesus into the manger and place him in the straw crib, while Mary and Joseph played the concerned birth parents.

The inner tube races went well the next afternoon; however, the thirty-degree temperature made Grandpa and Peter frequent the half-moon structure behind the hill. During one of their pit stops, Rod and Steve got buckets of water from a work pump shed, near the ravine, and poured it on the bottom of the hill to freeze.

They got everyone to agree they wouldn't tell. Meeting at the top of the hill for another run, Rod said, "Ok, Grandpa, Steve and I think we can beat you and Peter."

"You're on," he said.

The two inner tubes headed down hill at breakneck speed. It was a tie until Rod and Steve veered to the right halfway down, and Rod yelled, "Paybacks are hell, Grandpa."

Grandpa and Peter hit the ice at the bottom of the hill and shot toward the ravine. Peter screamed, "Grandpa!"

Grandpa hollered, "Geronimo."

The inner tube passed between two trees, like a jet banking in a narrow canyon, and flew into the depths of the small ravine. They all later learned that a Godsend of five-foot snowdrifts had accumulated against the back wall of the dry ravine bed.

Everyone ran to look, hoping that Peter and Grandpa were still alive. They all had visions of Grandma executing family members with a rolling pin.

To their surprise, Grandpa and Peter were holding each other in the snow bank and belly laughing about the best tube ride in the world. Then they started singing, We are the Champions.

It took awhile for the clan to amble back to the house. Grandpa had a hitch in his giddy-up. Grandma was waiting at the mud door with Jane. He could see her witch's-spell eye, and one, what am I going to do with you eye.

"And what excuse do you have this time?" she demanded.

Peter and Grandpa walked past her, heads held high, and said in unison, "We are the Champions of the world."

Dinner conversation was quite subdued until Rod and Steve confessed about the water and ice, with no little prompting from the other family members. The boys apologized to Grandma and explained they had no idea the inner tube would travel that far on ice. Nor, that there was a drop off to the ravine beyond the clump of trees. The boys emphasized that Grandpa did not appear to be Tarzan.

The meal—no crow eaten—became edible for everyone. The grandkids had pictured Grandpa sleeping on a cot in the basement if Rod and Steve hadn't come clean.

Dinner concluded; Jim called. "I'll be able to fly in tomorrow, Grandpa, and stay a week during school break."

No sooner had he hung up than Laura called and indicated they would be there tomorrow, late morning.

The next day, Clay picked Jim up at the airport. By the time they got back to the house—last minute shopping for Grandma thrown in—Laura, Bill, and family were there. Laura was happy Jim would be able to stay for the new Christmas. It had been seven years since she had seen him face to face, after he went to live with his father.

After lunch, the whole family helped Laura and Bill with the remaining displays. Laura decided on one of the carriage house horse stalls for the manger scene. The preliminary work completed; everyone worked on equipment for the toboggan races.

That afternoon the shaded side of the slope had the most new powder from the night before. The toboggans waxed; teams were chosen. Family members could be on the same team if they wanted. Grandpa got to pick and choose.

There were four toboggans: two four-seaters, one six-seater, and Grandpa's eight-seater. With the largest family, Clay had a distinct advantage and, since toboggans ran faster with all the seats filled, Grandpa got runs with grandkids as an equalizer. He made sure that Joseph, Peter, and Mary got to spend race time on his toboggan. He added Jim, Steve, and Pam for ballast. Everyone would have six runs. The team with the longest run would win Grandma's jam cake and a one month pass to a movie theater. The only caveat to the races was that Grandpa wouldn't go to the outhouse. He went to a clump of trees near the creek and kept a jaundiced eye on the slope.

On the sixth run, Grandpa's team sailed past Clay's best mark—Grandpa loved jam cake.

The next day, twenty runs: ten in the morning, ten in the afternoon. The winning team members would each get a new Rolex and a one-month coupon for pizzas.

The competition was close. Clay's team was declared the winner after the twentieth run. They were congratulated by being tossed into the ravine snowdrift.

"We're still ticking," Clay yelled from the snow bank, pointing to his wrist where the new watch would go.

The new Christmas Day will be a treat to last a lifetime, Grandpa mused, when they got back to the house.

The neighbor was ready to come by with the sleigh and caribou. Two of Goodwin's friends had placed special presents in the basement storage room. They'd arrived in a grocery-wood-delivery truck, while the families were on the hill, giving the appearance they were bringing items for the family dinners.

Grandpa, Clay, Bill, Dick, and all the grandkids went out early on the train to plug in the Christmas displays at their sidings. With all the family there that would be coming for the holidays, the displays and lights were turned on. The train was a hit; three go-arounds requested. The first round: high-speed—snow flying—basement cot looming in the engineer's mind.

Grandma, Jane, Laura, Hunny, and Rosemary helped prepare the Christmas Eve meal: cinnamon crust, multiple loaves of home-baked bread, and six apple pies. Last, but not least, the hamlogna.

Clay, Peter, Jim, Pam, and Grandpa fixed batches of assorted candies and taffy from old family recipes. Each grandchild took turns going outside to churn the ice cream. The traditional eve meal was coming together for the family.

After the taffy was laid out on the marble countertop by the kitchen sink, Grandpa had the back door and kitchen door propped open. Clean hands coated in butter, the family was divided in half. The taffy was folded ten times then both teams grabbed an end and started to pull. Stumbling over each other and laughing, Jane and Clay's team won. New record: thirty-six feet before the taffy broke.

At dinner, the toboggan winners were announced and toasted. Laura and family surprised everyone by winning the first three afternoon races. Bill had a great racing technique. However, Clay's family had taken the all day event by wearing everyone down.

Clay couldn't resist chiding Jane for not having more team members.

Jane's rebuttal was a little more hurtful than fun when she said, "At least I get to see all my kids grow up."

Grandpa and Peter tried to lighten the moment by singing one verse of, We are the Champions. But the damage had been done.

Laura said, "Let's not go there tonight. This time is for Mom and Dad."

Clay got up to leave the table.

"Everyone has burdens to bear, son," Mother said. "Don't be so sensitive."

"I'm going for a walk," Clay said.

"I'll go with you," Sunny added.

"Don't be late for Santa," Grandpa cautioned. "He may be here within the hour."

"I'll probably see him before y'all do," Clay responded. He and Sunny headed for the front door.

The family cleared the dishes and watched as dusky snow mounded on the sills and peered in the kitchen windows. "What a beautiful sight," Grandma said.

"Hark!" Grandpa said. "Is that Santa I hear?"

Everyone made a mad dash, out the front door and onto the veranda, in time to see Santa in his lighted sleigh pulled by six caribou—bells peeling. Santa waved to everyone and tossed something to Clay.

Everyone was ecstatic; they had seen a great spectacle. When Clay and Sunny came up on the veranda, he had a leather bound book in his hand.

"What did Santa give you, Dad?" Rod asked.

Clay was misty eyed when he handed it to Rod and Steve and said, "Santa said it's for your two boys."

Rod and Steve looked at the gold leaf title: Book of Memories. They knew a group hug was in order by everyone on the veranda. When everyone turned to go in the house there wasn't a dry eye to be found.

After a round of hot chocolate, Laura had Hunny and

Rosemary get in their angel outfits for the important presentation of Jesus to the manger.

They all proceeded to the carriage house with their candles and went to the stall, awaiting the baby. Mary and Joseph, playing their parts, looked forlorn, as though they knew ahead of time the end result of the miraculous birth. Hunny and Rosemary came forward looking like angels, all in white, carrying the baby in swaddling cloth. Laura, with lighted candles in each hand, was their guiding light. When Jesus was placed in the straw crib, they all recited the Lords Prayer. The babe smiled back at the family, and Grandma started singing Silent Night.

Mary took a small blanket, draped on her arm, and covered the child. They all walked silently out of the carriage house latching the doors, securing the baby from the outside world.

Jim, Rod and Steve were assigned to distribute presents from under the tree and bring the special gifts from the basement. Everyone, without exception, received one gift of a lifetime: college tuition assistance, Europe on a shoestring, plane ticket accounts for Rod, Steve and Jim, in addition to new laptop computers.

"Grandma and I decided that we can't take it with us. We wanted to see the family enjoy things while we're still here. The bigger items will be available in your hometown at your store of choice."

Everyone was still in shock when Rod, Steve, and Jim brought up three, mockup HD televisions, and gave one to each family. Everyone but Grandpa started crying, until he said, "If it makes all of you that sad, I'll send it all back." Instantly the crying stopped, except for Grandma.

The evening was spent playing games, drinking hot toddies and cider, and singing around the piano. Grandma got her wish, when Grandpa played a flawless rendition of Jingle Bells and White Christmas.

"This special moment took forever to find and will be gone on the morrow," Grandma said.

"We should do this again real soon," Laura said.

"Yes." They all said in unison. "Let's do this again."

As sleep sprinkled on most eyelids, Mother and Laura were still at the kitchen table watching the snowfall. "How are you, Mom?"

"I'm holding my own. Some days are better than others. Really wish I could shake this disease for good."

"I don't know how to say this," Laura said, her voice quivering, "but here goes. I wish we could go back in time and start many areas of our lives over, but we can't. I have so much to be sorry for and so much to be thankful for. Most of all, I've waited a long time to tell you how much I love you, and I know how much you love me and always did. That's why it kills me to tell you and Dad that Bill and I are starting a home business and can't take on any more responsibility right now." Laura began to cry, stood and started toward the window.

Getting out of her chair, she took Laura in her arms and held her as gently as the day she was born, knowing the moment would last a lifetime.

* * * *

The next two days were spent catching up on lives and goals, coupled with past memories, photo albums, and great toboggan and inner tube races. But the real world rang in with each phone call, e-mail, Facebook or text, and everyone knew it was time to leave.

The third morning was goodbye day. Grandpa, seeing Rod, Jim, and Steve draw back from the families, called everyone together for a hug in the snow.

Grandma walked up to the three boys huddled together and said, "Love stretches beyond all bounds."

She kissed each boy on the lips, giving gentle grandma hugs.

They all began to tear-up again until Grandpa yelled, "Last one to make a snow angel is a rotten egg."

The fallout was quick and almost complete. Hunny lost. She didn't want snow on her clothes and hair.

Clay and Laura agreed they had room to carry all the boys to the airport, with Clay quipping in a jovial way, "And save the old man a trip in the snow."

He stood on the front veranda with his best friend, and waved goodbye to the last of the kids and grandkids as they drove away. "A perfect ending to the best and only Christmas with the whole family since the kids left home," he said.

"To tell the truth, I really hoped for a little more reconciliation on our kids part." Her voice choked back tears. "You'd have thought after all this time Jane and Clay would quit—"

He cut her off. "All very normal for most families, especially ours."

"I know, I know," she said with a forlorn look.

"But it still hurts. They're supposed to be closer as family; yet, they act like they're complete strangers sometimes."

"I think it's time to go inside by the fire. There's a wind coming up, and you don't want to get chilled."

They went about putting the decorations away exactly as they had found them. The grandkids had helped put all the outside decorations and displays away before they left.

Late that afternoon the phone rang; it was Jane. "The family and I had a wonderful time, Mom. Tell Dad I even had fun with Clay on the slopes. I hope it made your holiday wish come true."

"It did. And I'll tell Dad. Thanks for helping me."

"Gotta go." The phone clicked off.

"Just like Jane to be first," she said.

He quipped, "They have portable phones today, Mother. Besides, this isn't a competition."

She began to laugh, then the coughing started. She didn't want to think about cancer, and told herself to knock it off. However, she could only think of Jane's competitive nature to be in control, and how that had proven to be a blessing and an albatross.

"Are we guessing who will call next?" he asked, holding her until the coughing spell passed.

"Clay, of course."

"Oh, he'll drive like mad; scaring everyone in and outside the car until he gets home. Then, when they get all the luggage unloaded and in the house, I bet he'll go to bed and forget he told you that he would call first thing."

She patted his hand, "Wishful thinking on my part."

"I actually think Laura will call next. She was awfully moody when she left. I had a few positive words with her and it seemed to perk her up. The older she's gotten, the more intelligent old dad has gotten. What do you think?"

"I guess it's not really important," she said, evading the question, "who does or doesn't call first. They all said they had a good time, but only Laura said let's do it again and meant it."

He tried to fend off her partial hurt by stating the obvious: "We don't really have to worry about this anymore, do we?"

"No," she said. "We don't have to worry about it. However, I do think it interesting that Laura's kids said their sweaters wouldn't fit and would we please exchange them and bring their new ones when we come to visit."

"That was unusual. I really thought we had the sizes right."

That afternoon, Laura called. "Mom, I just want to tell you and Dad how much fun we had. Bill and the kids are still talking about it. I am so grateful you flew Jim in for the reunion. And what a great setting you found for Christmas and New Years."

"Your dad found this place. I'll tell him. It was wonderful to have y'all, and you seem to be doing so well. I'm thankful we had our talk. You've come a long way."

The next morning during breakfast, Clay called. "Yes, Dad, I went right to bed when I got home. I was exhausted, but I wanted you and Mom to know the family reunion was better than I thought it would be. I was tickled to have the boys there. I can't thank y'all enough."

They spent the rest of the daylight hours enjoying the home and each other, while making sure everything was left as they had found it.

After securing the house, they went out the front door, locked it, and placed the key in the magnet box that attached to a metal plate on the bottom of the porch swing. They paused to gaze out over the fresh dusting of snow. He held out his arm, and they went down the front steps.

They started toward the carriage house where their truck was parked. "This will always be the best of all our Christmases," she said.

"What a great gift to the kids and grandkids," he said.

She turned to him, squeezed his hand and said, "I love you, forever."

"And I love you," he whispered as they kissed. "You have the softest lips."

He had her hold his arm tightly so she wouldn't fall as they ambled—each admiring the other as if for the first time.

The carriage house doors moaned. Opening them wide enough for the two of them to slip inside, he closed the doors behind them. There was enough light from the moon to enable them to get into the truck.

The rubber hose had been attached after lunch and piped into the back sliding window. He always left the keys in the ignition. Not paying much attention to anything in the dark except his arm around his best friend, he started the truck.

While the toxic fumes filled the truck, he held her close and kissed her one last time. She laid her head on his shoulder and he tilted his head back, while his mind made one last trip over all their preparations for this event, hoping all the bases had been covered: the wills, letters of explanation to each child and grandchild that would be sent out after. It wasn't that they were trying to be selfish. Illness was taking a toll, and the kids were busy with their own lives.

"We should say the Lord's prayer together and ask for forgiveness for what we're about to do—kind of an insurance policy," he said.

After the prayer she whispered, "He'll understand. He died so we wouldn't have to suffer the way he did."

The fumes were making him groggy and giving him a headache. He tilted his head forward, opened his eyes and saw what looked like a piece of tattered Christmas wrapping draped on the dash behind the steering wheel. He didn't remember putting anything there.

He forced himself to knife out his hand and arm cutting through a foggy mind. Retrieving the paper, he tried to discern what was on it. Bleary eyes saw the words Grandpa and Grandma. Startled, he turned off the engine, forced himself out of the truck, opened the passenger door and got her out to fresh air.

Her coughing had kept her awake longer than expected. It took thirty to forty-five minutes for their coughing and headaches to lessen. Drinking in the cool fresh air, she finally said, "What happened?"

"I found a note from the grandkids on the dash, and couldn't go through with it."

"Are you sure?" she said between coughs.

"Yes. You have to hear this: 'Grandma and Grandpa, we had a ball. We love you forever. See you next year,' signed by all the grandkids."

"We should try hard not to disappoint them."

Holding her close, he said, "I agree. And would you look at that bright star in the heavens. Must be showing us our way home."

"True," she said with a glint in her weary eyes. "And a child shall lead us."

"One more time for the grandkids?" he said.

"Yes. God willing," she said. "One more time."

The Crystal Christmas Tree

Julie, ten, and Butch, eleven, didn't want to think about the 2009 Christmas holidays. They knew they couldn't expect much in the way of presents, if they received anything. While other kids in the Fayetteville schools looked forward with anticipation to what they were going to get for Christmas, Julie and Butch could only think about where they'd soon be living, and what they would or wouldn't have to eat.

After their mom, Ann Pearson, was laid off during the recession, the family had made it two months in the apartment before the landlord said that he couldn't let them live there any longer without paying full rent. As a single parent, with determination, and no support network, Ann had to make a difficult choice.

A frigid November morning, she and the children packed all their belongings into a few suitcases and Walmart bags and moved onto the streets. They tried to stay at shelters, but Butch was too old to stay with the women, and too young to stay in the men's shelter. Bentonville had the proper facilities, but due to distance and transportation issues it wasn't an option. She obtained a tent with sleeping bags, and the family settled in the wooded area south of the Sallie near Walker Park. Six weeks into their barren existence, Ann's ex-boss, Louise, spotted them in the park, when she brought grandkids to play.

"Ann, why don't you and the kids come home with me?" Louise said. "I've got an empty cottage house in my backyard. You can stay there for a while and get the kids off the street."

"I can't thank you enough," Ann said. "I've been worried about the kids, and what they must think living this way."

That evening, after Ann and the children were cleaned up,

Louise fixed a pot of stew and homemade bread for her grandkids and Ann's family. They all ate like there was no tomorrow.

Later, as Ann and her kids prepared for bed, it dawned on her that where they were at that very moment had been a pipedream only the day before.

The following morning at breakfast, Anne's family looked different: bathed, rested, and dressed in washed clothes. Louise said, "Would you like to use my computer. I know of an online secretarial site you might be interested in working."

"I'll try anything," Ann said. "I can't thank you enough for this blessing, but if we're a burden—"

"Thirty-two years ago, my first husband was killed in a car wreck. I was emotionally at rock bottom. We were young, no insurance, and had too much debt. A friend reached out to me and saved my life. Now I can pay it forward."

The following week Ann's children started back to school full-time. And on the way home the last day before Christmas break, they found a twelve-inch, discarded tree on top of a trashcan. The tiny branches, almost bare of plastic needles, were shaped around a green and red plaid covered, cardboard cone, topped with a bent, faded, gold star. All their classmates had been blind to the discarded tree.

"Mom. Hey, Mom," Julie yelled, as she and her brother burst in the door. "See what Butch and I found on our way home?"

"What a nice tree," she said. "It was probably left for us. Where would you like to put it?"

"There on the little table near the front window. We can decorate it, and—"

Ann interrupted. "I don't think anyone will see it back here."

"The angels that brought us here will see it," Julie said.

Startled by the beautiful sentiment of her daughter, Ann felt a lump of tears forming in her throat and opened her arms. Butch and Julie rushed over; Ann pulled them both in to a mother bear hug.

"You're absolutely correct. We'll look around and find something bright to decorate it with for the angels."

That evening, sitting around a yellowed, Formica table after decorating the tree with a single strand of tiny white lights and paper cut-out decorations, Ann said, "Money will be tight this Christmas. What if we get creative and find discarded items for Christmas presents and give them to each other."

"That's a great idea," Butch said. "I'm sure all the presents would appreciate a new home."

"I agree," Julie said. "It can be a treasure hunt."

Butch was first to locate a gift: a Raggedy-Ann doll, one pigtail and one eye missing, rested in a cardboard box on the curb, next to a chipped, miniature, tea set.

"Mom," he said, walking in the front door. "Look what I found for Julie."

Two days later, Julie found a skateboard with a wheel missing and a one-paddle Wii set, which she took to her mother. "Look what I found for Butch?"

Ann rejoiced with the thought and direction of the Christmas treasures concept, and the next day decided to tell Louise. "And I'm impressed with the kids and the thoughtfulness they're putting into this," she concluded.

"I think it's a great idea," Louise said. "I'll mention it during the monthly block-party meeting tonight and recommend the whole housing tract think about participating in the project for Christmas."

"What can we do if the treasures are broken or need repair, like the one's I have now?" Ann asked.

"Wally, next door, does small repair work as a hobby," Louise said. "He needs something besides that big house to keep him busy, since he retired, and his wife died. There's also my handyman, William, who does my yard work and can fix anything. I'll contact both of them today and see if they'll help."

"Now I have to start looking for treasures," Ann said. "—Oh, Louise, I really want to thank you for the hospitality and use of your computer. I'm starting to get referrals."

"You're more than welcome, Ann. You'll never know how bad I felt when I had to let you go at work . . . seniority and all that. Never think that you weren't doing a good job. You were. Even with three of you gone, everyone left, including myself, had to take a pay cut."

"I know that now, Louise. The initial shock takes the wind out of your sails; especially when you're single and have kids that depend on you. I did love working for you."

"Enough of the pre-Christmas blues talk; let's focus on what's going right with us both," Louise said. "Come to think of it, I'm sure there's stuff in the attic and closets of this old house, and stored in part of the barn, but I can't begin to tell you what's there. I'd bet there're items from generations ago. We'll have to have a treasure hunt."

"Let me know when you want to start and I'll help."

"I'll know more after the meeting here this evening. Would you like to come and meet the neighbors? Oh, Ann. That would be even better; you could make the pitch."

"I'm not really part of the neighborhood." Her chagrin expression spoke volumes.

"You are, if I say you are," Louise said. A cheek popping smile melted any concerns.

"When is it?" Ann asked.

"Seven tonight. Don't be late. You're my greeter."

"That gives me time to clean up and fix the kids some supper. See you then."

Ann put on her only remaining dress and walked to the front door, rang the bell, and let herself in. "I'm here, Louise."

"Go on into the parlor; I'll be down in a minute," came a voice from upstairs.

The Chippendale mahogany furniture, arranged precisely in the room, appeared designed for the exact placement. "I love the furniture," Louise said, entering the room. "I inherited this house and furnishings from an uncle who never had children. He and his wife travelled for his work. They both died in a plane crash, and for some reason he thought I would be the one to care enough to fix it up to the grand state it once was. He was right. With the help of Wally and William and the construction background I learned from my father, I've been able to restore this home at minimal cost. I've even helped Wally next door with his restorations."

The doorbell rang. Ann said, "I'll get it for you."

She opened the door; eight men and women stepped through the doorway, shook hands and greeted her with their names. She was taken aback and barely uttered a welcome, much less her name.

Louise brought in a tray of tea, cakes, and English biscuits.

Once everyone was served, Louise addressed the group. "Not all of you know this, but Ann used to work for me, and, I had to lay her off. As a single parent and unemployed, she and her two children ended up on the street. I found them recently and brought them here to the cottage house. She's been working online and is doing well while she gets re-started. However, they don't have much money, and that is what presented a very creative idea. They decided to find discarded items and toys and try to fix them so they could give them to each other as gifts. A small, discarded, Christmas tree was the impetus. Wally and William have agreed to help with the rebuilding and mechanical aspects."

Wally spoke up, "We could try to spread the idea throughout the whole neighborhood. I know three families a block away who have kids that might enjoy the creative challenge. My wife would have loved this idea for Christmas. She always believed we all have treasures we tire of and someone else would cherish."

The vote was unanimous in favor of the Christmas concept. Once every family that agreed to participate was in the pool, names would be drawn, family members introduced, and they could get to know each other.

Three days later, fifteen families had signed up to participate, and the first meeting was to take place at Louise's house. The backgrounds of the families and members ranged from doctors to mechanics. Not everyone had children, but those that did had kids spanning all ages. It shouldn't be difficult to find one item that everyone would like to have or have fixed.

Wally was the one who came up with the unique idea of having the twelve days of Christmas like they celebrate in many foreign countries. The families voted and agreed. Home and neighborhood decorations would go up in time for the kickoff celebration on Christmas Day. Families drew names for their holiday responsibilities which included: preparations for the presentation of the child by Mary and Joseph; the manger families—including livestock, the shepherds and Maji families. One gift for each participant per day would be given over the Epiphany season, and end with a collective dinner and celebration at Louise's house

As Christmas Day approached, the participating homes stood out on their respective streets like beacons in a dark sky. Some of the neighbors, who had initially declined to participate, now wanted to join the group. Louise contacted each family, explained the planning that had already taken place, and told them how they could start their own group this year. Next year there could be revisions and maybe streets could compete.

Wally and William had found that some of the children had a talent for rebuilding and creating gifts from discarded or broken items. They taught Butch how to repair a boat in a glass bottle. But he and Julie were still worried that they hadn't been able to find satisfactory gifts for their mother, though they had discovered clothes and some nice pots and pans that were in good shape.

Butch mentioned to Wally that he and Julie were having a hard time finding anything nice for their mother.

"I heard that your Mom needed newer software for her online work," Wally said. "My nephew takes in electronic equipment, rebuilds them and sells the items—everything from computers to cell phones. I've got him fixing one for your mother. Since you don't have anything yet, we can give her the computer together. You still need gifts for the other twelve days."

From the first meeting, the neighbors remarked that the residents had never been as sociable and agreeable. Even those who had been living in their homes most of their lives couldn't believe the transition. One elderly member remarked to Wally that she hadn't felt the Christmas spirit in the neighborhood like this, since she was eight years old.

Louise gave Ann, Butch, and Julie permission to begin exploring the house, attic and barn, for gift items. The kids quickly located old trunks with clothes, quilts, shoes and pictures from another era, and smelled of mothballs or cedar wood. Old lamps, carved steamer trunks from Asia with ivory and jade figurines were also possible gifts.

Julie wandered into a darkened second floor bedroom, that didn't appear to have been used in years, and opened the drapes to let in sunlight. A small closet facing the window peaked her interest. Opening the door wide, something shone through a small crack in the back wooden panel, and she called Butch. Together they pulled and pushed until they found a lever that slid open the wall. Velvet covered shelves held beautiful jewelry and glass ornaments. "We better tell Mom and Louise about what we found today," Julie said. "Some of these things look expensive."

"I agree," Butch said. "Wouldn't these little glass pieces look pretty on our tree?"

Louise was shocked by what the kids had found in their treasure hunt. "I'm going to take the time to see what else is hidden in this house. Ann, you, Butch, and Julie can help me. I didn't know about the hidden shelves. What a treasure the kids found. Come to think of it, I had a letter once—that came with the will—that told me to look for all the wonderful treasures in this house. There may even have been a map. I don't remember. I was too busy working at the company and doing repairs at home. The place was quite rundown. I never took the time. The crystal glass ornaments the kids found are probably Swarovski. My mother had pieces also. Julie, I think you and Butch should take the small crystal ornaments and decorate your tree—and that Swarovski mouse is adorable."

The ornaments adorned the discarded tree and brought it to life. Neighbors came by nightly to see the crystal tree sparkling into the darkness.

Christmas came with singing and revelry. Wally, Louise and her other neighbors had hidden all the presents, preventing anyone from seeing them. The first treasures were exchanged and opened by all the participants at Louise's house. The exchange continued until the twelfth day after Christmas: Epiphany.

The neighborhood families had just finished opening their presents, and were sitting down for the last celebration meal, when the front doorbell rang. Louise answered the door.

"I'm John Ratcliff, a city inspector. I've been advised that you have been housing homeless people in your cottage out back. That violates the city ordinance for housing."

"I have a friend of mine and her children living here," Louise said. "She works online, and since she's in my care, she can't be constituted as homeless."

"I'm sorry, but the city ordinance doesn't allow for anyone except immediate family or relatives to live on your property. You do understand. We don't want multiple families like the Mexicans or minorities moving in together."

I'll be speaking to the mayor and city council tomorrow, Mr. Ratcliff. And as far as minorities go, would you like to come in and meet Dr. Vasquez and his family? As for me, my great, great, grandfather was Cherokee, and the land this neighborhood is built on was his. You need to check the city records and see who allowed the houses to be built in this area."

"I've already done that, ma'am. And your family lost all benefits and rights to the property when they allowed development. Three days and the squatters have to be out."

The dinner was a somber affair, and Ann thanked all the residents for their wonderful spirit and the best Christmas she and the kids had had since her husband died. Everyone piped in and said that they would do whatever they could to find a place for Ann and the kids. They definitely wanted them to come back for next Christmas and lead the party.

Wally asked a question out of the blue. "Do you know anything about your family tree, Ann?"

"A little. When I was very small, younger than Julie, I had a great aunt—a spinster from Lafayette, Indiana. She had a very unusual last name: Bozarth, if I'm not mistaken. Mom thought it was French, and said it was an old family name. My dad was named Alloway after his stepfather, and Pearson was my husband's name. We only visited my aunt a few times before she died. She was very old, but I never forgot the name."

"Small world. I'm a part-time genealogist and I've been trying to find a Bozarth from my family tree in the Midwest. Her first name didn't happen to be Marie, did it?"

The startled look on Ann's face said it all. "You mean we might be related?"

"I'll check my computer records tomorrow. I'd say there's a good chance."

Laughter and joy pulled up chairs and participated in the remaining festivities. They all felt Christmas wishes had been answered. Ann, however, knew it was going to be a sleepless night.

The next morning Louise, Ann, Butch, and Julie were having breakfast when a knock sounded, and the bell rang at the front door. Wally was standing there with an armful of papers when Louise opened the door.

"Come in, Wally. What have you got? Good news I hope?"

"Good news indeed," he said entering the kitchen. "Ann, you are from the Bozarth line of my family. How'd you and the kids like to come live in that big house of mine? It's been mighty lonely since Margret died. Maybe it's time to wake the walls up over there."

Ann started to cry. Butch and Julie moved to her and gave her a hug. "Does that mean we don't have to go live in the woods again?" Butch asked.

Wally put his arms around the three of them and said, "No family of mine will ever live on the streets."

"See, Mom," Julie said, hugging Wally's leg. "I told you the angels would see our tree!"

Rags of Angels

The Victorian structure stood dark this evening. The only sign of life, a dim porch bulb dangled from an open-wire socket in the ceiling above the front door. The light fixture had been missing ten years—not long after his wife died. And the peeling paint— edges curled like dirty, winter leaves—could relate to the loneliness in the home.

It used to be called the Gingerbread House. The smiling occupants had always added to the merriment of the neighborhood Christmas season: handing out assorted gingerbread treats for thirty years.

That's where this part of the story ends and another begins.

A light snow flitted through the tawny hue from the lone streetlamp and brought pause to the stoop-shouldered man in topcoat and galoshes—snow-shovel in hand. The sky had billowed large puffy flakes for two days, and he needed to clear a path from the house to the street.

"Where are you Mary?" he asked the heavenly flakes. "Are you warm enough in your favorite blanket I put in the casket?" The answer came in the tolling of St Catherine's bells for evening mass. "I hope you can bake there and handout those delicious gingerbread cookies. You did love Christmas."

"Who's Mary?" a child's voice asked from the shadowed sidewalk.

"Who said that?" he barked. Startled eyes searched for the voice. Where'd you come from? Go away! I've got work to do. Mary's none of your business. Who are you, anyway?"

"My name is John Paul Cielo. What's your name?" he asked, stepped from the shadows into the filtered light and extended a small, tattered-mitten hand. His clothes were frayed, ill-fitted hand-me-downs with a tattered, rainbow-colored scarf.

"I don't shake hands with strangers who come out of the dark and ask questions they aren't supposed to ask. Besides, my name is none of your business. Where's your family, anyway? You look too young to be out on the street in this weather."

"I'm trying to find the right place to help Mom. She's been sick lately and can't get well. We haven't been in town long. Sort of passing through. There's my mom, Ruth, my little brother, David, and me. My dad died in Iraq, but he and mom weren't married, so she gets no support. Can I clear a path for you for a few dollars?"

"No! I'll do it myself. Everybody has a sob story around Christmas, and I've heard all I want to hear. Now, be on your way so I can finish. I'm getting cold standing out here, and the snow's piling up."

Scooping a shovel full of snow, he heard the voice trail into the dark, "Sorry I bothered you, mister. I hope you have enough light."

Ten more scoops and his breathing labored, muscles burned. *The doctor would shoot me if he saw me out here. Oh, well, you can't live forever.*

He dragged the shovel up the front steps and placed it by the broken porch handrail, then stomped the snow from his galoshes. One last glance at the partial path and voiceless sidewalk, he opened the door and entered the foyer. Using his boot puller, he slipped off the rubbers and left them on the worn entry mat: "Love Resides Here". The saying had been his wife's favorite.

He stared at the last remnants of the way life used to be and said, "Not any more, Mary."

Morning brought little relief from the snowdrifts. The paper was nowhere to be seen when he ventured onto the porch. The partial path cleared yesterday was completely covered again, and the news on the radio was for another week of moderate snow. The snow continued to prevent him from shopping or walking anywhere. Hurrying inside, he said, "The last time it snowed like this, Mary, was the year we were married. Remember when the heat and electricity went out for a week. It was four days before the Red Cross could help us."

Whap! "What could that be?" he said, and returned to the front door. Squinting through the beveled-glass, he saw the paper by the door. Stepping outside, the cold wind rushed inside his pajamas and gave him the same bone-chill he felt when Mary was lowered in the ground. Scooping up the paper, he caught movement out of the corner of his eye. The little boy from last night had his hand up and was waving while walking away.

What was his name? John something?

Tipping the paper in the boy's direction was the closest thing to thank you he had given anyone in the last ten years.

Morning sidled by—still no clear path. His chest had been hurting. "What do you think, Mary? Time for me to come visit?"

The hall clock answered: striking 2:00 p.m. Mary's grandfather had built the clock from scratch—works to wood— and she cherished it more than all the treasures acquired in her worldly travels. The old man had told her the clock would last five lifetimes.

"I would have gladly given it away for free, if I could have kept you for one lifetime, Mary."

The knock on the front door startled him; he wasn't expecting company. His neighbors knew better than to drop in unannounced.

"Everyone knows they have to call ahead," he said, on the way to the door. Peering through the glass, no one appeared to be there. Knock. Knock. There it was again.

Twisting the knob, he jerked the door open, charged out and found John Paul sitting at the side of the door. "What's the matter with you, boy? You could have caused me to have a heart attack."

"I really need to help my mom and brother. Your walk is still full of snow. Can't I clear a path for you? It's almost Christmas."

"Okay! Okay! I do need the path cleared or the mailman won't deliver. No meals-on-wheels either, and I haven't been feeling well. Wait a minute, this is a school day; don't you go to school?"

"I'm home schooled."

"Where do you live?"

"Over by the highway."

"Where...over by the highway?"

"I'll tell you, if you tell me your name."

He paused while considering his options then said, "My name is Harold Lloyd Burton III. Now, where do you live?"

"We're staying in an abandoned barn, in a field near the highway."

"Stay here and I'll get the shovel." A banished-warmth inside him started to awaken,

when he returned to the porch.

Shovel-in-hand, John Paul finished a path in thirty minutes. Returning to the porch, he rang the bell. Mr. Burton came to the door with a five-dollar bill in hand and said, "You're a hard worker...John Paul is it?"

"Yes, sir."

"You said your mother was sick. How bad is she?"

"I think it's her heart. She can't breathe well, and her chest hurts."

Running filthy fingers through his disheveled hair, he said, "Mary loved Christmas and would lend a hand to anyone who asked her. It's been so lonely without her all these years. I've forgotten her spirit." His eyes misting, a sad voice asked, "Do you know him, Mary?"

It took a few minutes for Mr. Burton to compose himself. A half-hearted smile creased his lips when, "I'll tell you what. I'll check on a place to help your mother, and you can consider working part time for me. I've got odd jobs I can't do anymore and it's been ten years since I had anyone work on this house. We'll take it one day at a time. Be here tomorrow morning, nine sharp. If you like the place I've got in mind, you can bring your mom and brother tomorrow afternoon.

Turning to leave, John Paul said, "Would you look at the beautiful flakes coming down. It's as though we're in a dome and the sky is alive."

"By the way," Mr. Burton called after him. "How old did you say you were?"

"I didn't say. But I really appreciate your help for my mom and brother. I'm twelve."

The next morning, the appointment time came and went—no John Paul. The scourge of sorrow seeped back into his being. He ruminated, "Maybe they moved on, Mary. Probably for the best."

Retrieving the newspaper, he built a fire in the pink-marbled, living room fireplace and sat down in his favorite rocker to read.

Joy dragged itself back down the basement and waited silently in a dark corner.

He rocked, oblivious to the words in the paper, his mind flirting with times past. The hours toiled as the fire succumbed to ashes and firefly embers. The Grandfather clock struck twelve. A faint knock followed by two harder knocks. It sounded like it came from the back porch.

He ambled to the back door and watched as a tuft of hair floated along the bottom edge of the leaded-glass window. He

51

could see John Paul standing there, but the junk-strewn backyard looked cleaner.

Jerking the door open, he said, "Come inside, it's too cold for me to stand out there." Closing the door, the flood of questions started: "Where have you been? Why didn't you come at nine? Why—"

"Busy," John Paul answered. "I'm finding there's more work this time of year I have to attend to, especially with Mom sick. I got here after nine and started cleaning up the backyard. You have a nice building out there, and a great area for a greenhouse. The earth looks good and should grow wonderful plants."

Mr. Burton looked out and said with a sigh, "You did a good job, John Paul, but I thought you weren't coming back. How did you know there'd been a greenhouse? Mary had had one many years ago."

"When I picked up the tools and trash covering the ground, it was easy to see the earth and the foundation of a greenhouse. Your big garage held all of the tools and equipment that needed to be put up . . . plenty of room to spare. A place like that could keep three people out of the cold, but it looks like someone has been using it and hasn't been back in a while."

"That was Mary's studio," he said with a note of reverence. "She loved to paint. Some local town folks bought a few of her paintings before she died, but after her death I covered the rest up and left them in the studio. Art people came around later and asked about more paintings, but I told them there weren't anymore. I didn't want them bothering me; it's all I have left of her. That's when I hung her large self-portrait over the living-room mantle. Every Christmas Eve, I go out to the studio, stoke up the potbelly with wood and spend time with the paintings. I love the one she called: The Hands of God. Two hands, palms up, extended through black clouds, cradling our daughter, Maddie— drawn toward a white light, bright as the brightest star. She died when she was your age—Christmas Eve. Mary never was the same after Maddie's death, and The Hands was her last painting. I've always believed Mary died of a broken heart." He buried his face in his hands and cried out, "God help me, I miss them so!"

John Paul helped him into an old wooden chair, put a hand on his shoulder and whispered, "Peace be with you this Christmas."

Mr. Burton felt a great weight lifted, but he wasn't sure what he would find to fill the void.

Joy moved from the dark basement corner and started up the stairs.

Mr. Burton regained his composure and said, "I want to show you something upstairs; then I want you to go get your mother and brother."

On the way to the staircase, they passed a large shelf-lined room filled with dusty books. John Paul asked, "May I use your library sometime? I can clean the room while I look for my favorite book. I love to read, and maybe I can find a copy there."

"Yes, of course. Maddie loved that room and traveled all over the world in those books."

John Paul helped steady him as they proceeded up the winding mahogany staircase and entered the first door on the left. The bedroom was filled with remembrances of a little girl: Rag dolls; a quilted rag bedspread; a picture of her dog, Rags; a rag pillow cover with a centered picture of her in a rag-tag hat, and a miniature playhouse adorned with rag features.

"Mary couldn't bring herself to come in here after her death. Oh, we talked of having a memorial made for her, but we never did. Then Mary started painting more, until she got ill. I've often thought of having a memorial wall hanging made from all the items Maddie loved, and hang it near the portrait of her mother. But, I'm tired. Sorry, I've taken up enough of your time. Why don't you go get your mom and brother, and I'll go fire up the potbelly in the studio?"

When John Paul returned to the studio-garage with Ruth and David, day was drawing down. Mr. Burton was startled to see that they were more poorly dressed than John Paul. David was a small child, swaddled in worn out clothes. Ruth wore a moth-eaten coat over her ratty looking clothes. Her old shoes were wrapped much like pictures of Washington's men at Valley Forge.

Coughing out a thank you, she neared the stove rubbing her hands together. "It's been a while since we felt warmth like this," she said. "So much coldness in the world. We can't thank you enough. How can we repay you?"

"Do you know how to sew?" he asked. "I need to find someone to make a memorial wall piece for me."

"Why, yes I can. I worked as a seamstress before I got sick. Give me a little time to warm up and replenish my energy. Do you have a sewing machine I can use?"

"I still have one," he said. "I started many times to get rid of it, but couldn't bring myself to do it. Mary loved to sew and quilt before Maddie died. I also called some of my neighbors, whom I startled, I'm sure, and told them of your plight. They offered to help with food for the holidays. There are two cots and an easy chair in here. Sometimes Mary would work late, and I'd come out and spend time with her. Tomorrow I'll see to another cot. I brought out blankets, and there's plenty of wood to keep the stove going. Here's a picnic basket with some hot soup from my next-door neighbor. I'll see everyone in the morning."

"Sleep well, Mr. Burton . . . and Merry Christmas," John said. A cherub-smile warmed the wanton corners of the studio.

The next morning, Mr. Burton came to the studio and noticed Ruth looked and sounded healthier; the cough had all but vanished overnight. "Breakfast is ready in the house," he said. "There's plenty of hot water, and everyone can get cleaned up. I would say wash your clothes, but they would probably fall apart. I'm sure we can find some new clothes for everyone."

While he walked back to the house, he pondered how people could live in rags, and not have a more pungent aroma about them. Rather, the scent of innocence—like the first breath of a cleansed newborn—wafted around them.

They were gathered around the kitchen table when the initial banging and scrapping on the house startled Mr. Burton. Going out the front door, he found neighbors working on his porch and replacing the broken light fixture. He wished them a Merry Christmas, returned to the breakfast table and asked, "Did you know about this, John Paul?"

"A kindness given is a kindness received," he said. "Your neighbors have seen your worthiness and come to help."

With the meal finished, Ruth asked, "May I see the sewing room and material?"

"Right this way," Mr. Burton said, pushing himself up from the spindle-backed chair and shuffling toward an adjoining room. The fireplace had been started earlier, and the chill was gone.

They all worked together to remove the coverings and minimize the dust in the air. The bolts of beautiful material and spools of colored thread cast a rainbow hue through musty sunshine. It was obvious the room had not been occupied in years. A commercial sewing machine, protected by a dust cover, stood centered in the room.

"There is more than enough material to make a memorial and some new clothes. Is there anything specific you want in it?" Ruth asked.

"I would like a little piece of everything Maddie loved, plus the picture of her on the pillow cover to be the centerpiece," he said.

The next two days were filled with the festive noise of

neighbors working on the house. John Paul ran errands, went to the library to read, and helped with his brother. Mr. Burton went to the barbershop with a neighbor and began to clean himself up for the first time in years. He even took out the recipes to prepare Mary's favorite gingerbread cookies.

Joy climbed back up the stairs and settled in the portrait with Mary.

Ruth enjoyed the long work hours and appeared to gain strength. She'd started the memorial by setting the background: a centered, bright star near the top, a sun and moon in each corner, and a picture of Maddie made from pieces and rags, in an overlay pattern on the pillowcase. Next, multiple birds and sea creatures were added. Early morning Christmas Eve day, Ruth added a pieced appliqué of Mr. Burton on one side of Maddie, and Mary on the other. Her dog, Rags, was placed under her picture. The finished montage portrayed the world as she emerged from it.

Ruth finished the memorial in time to make some new clothes for the three of them.

When Mr. Burton came home from shopping Christmas Eve, a neighbor helped him into the house with two full bags of toys. They even brought in a Christmas tree and lights and placed it in the living room so Mary could see it. He hadn't noticed the memorial hanging on the wall, not far from Mary's portrait, until he was on the ladder and the star was ready to be placed on the top of the tree. Stunned, he looked around and saw the beaming smiles in the room and promised himself he wouldn't break down. He finished placing the star, climbed down and crossed the room to touch the piece.

"This is like having them back again," he said. "I can't thank you enough."

The doorbell chimed. "Who could that be on Christmas Eve?"

When he opened the door, Mayor Wright and two townspeople, who had purchased paintings, stood there. He said,

"You must have heard I'm going to attempt to make gingerbread cookies to pass cut, but you're early, or, are you here to carol?"

"Neither," Mayor Wright said. "We're here to offer Mary's paintings a permanent home. They'll never leave our community, and you can visit anytime. The few she sold have become world famous. There are millions of art lovers who want to see her work. She will live on forever."

"I don't understand. How did you find out I had more paintings?"

"An anonymous message was left at my office, stating we might find more Mary Burton paintings in a studio behind your house."

Mr. Burton glanced at her portrait and asked, "Is that what you want, Mary?"

Joy smiled.

"You may send the art director to pick them up tomorrow. Tonight she stays with me for the last time," he said, closing the door. Loneliness was left standing on the doorstep.

He turned to John Paul. "I wonder who could have told them about the paintings?"

John Paul beamed, "I cannot tell a lie. I did. I believe you know Mary would have wanted that."

"In that case, let's have something to eat and open presents."

After supper, everyone huddled around the tree. Ruth said, "Why don't we sing some carols and end with Hark The Hearld Angels Sing?"

Mr. Burton couldn't believe he remembered any of the songs. The words were inexplicably in his memory, though locked away all those many years.

When the carols ended, John Paul said, "We'll be leaving tomorrow. It's a day of rest, and we must move on."

"But I have presents for all of you. Can't you open them and take them with you?"

"It would make us happy if you gave them to your neighbors and their kids for helping you. We travel light."

"At least let me give you a book to read in your home studies. I have hundreds. What is your favorite? And, if I don't have it, I'll get it for you."

"I really don't need a copy," John Paul said. "I've read it so many times, I know it by heart. I found and read it again in your library. Thank you, anyway. Why don't you use the studio tonight, and that way you can be with Mary? We'll be preparing to leave and get some sleep in here."

"You will wait for me to say goodbye, won't you?"

"We'll wait. We don't have far to go."

Christmas morning arrived with large dancing flakes and red-cheeked children playing in the snow. John Paul knocked on the studio door and waited as a bleary eyed Mr. Burton came to the door. "Time for us to go, Mr. Burton. Thank you for everything. Mother always feels better when she's around joy and kindness."

Ruth, David and John Paul started across the yard and heard him yell, "Wait, John Paul, you never told me the name of your favorite book."

The wind must have drowned out part of the response. He could swear he heard him say, "Genesis."

The Homeless Snowman

Cleveland, Ohio had been hit hard by the recession, and as the 1974 Christmas season approached, joy packed its skimpy bags of cheer and moved under a local bridge.

Bill Mason, highly decorated Vietnam veteran, had found it virtually impossible to adjust to civilian life and hold down a job after returning home from the conflict. Besides showing the affects of Agent Orange, he had a deep-seated PTSS: Post Traumatic Stress Syndrome—the tunnel rat in him had never crawled out of his brain.

His family stuck by him when he returned home and tried to make sure he got the help needed. But the military was reluctant to agree that Agent Orange, or four combat tours, contributed to any of Bill's maladies. The public's negative reaction to returning soldiers from Vietnam exacerbated the already tentative family plight.

Bill, his wife and two children spiraled onto the streets and into the homeless lifestyle, seeking food and shelter as best they could. Six months after hitting the streets, while everyone but Bill slept in an abandoned commercial building, a fire wiped out his family and five other vagrant vets. Bill had survived by scavenging for early discards at food establishments.

His war record write-up in the press initially got him the medical help he needed, and got him off the streets. Three months later, it was as though the military tired of trying to help. The local veteran hospital psychiatrists wrote in their reports that Bill didn't appear to be trying to help himself.

Fed up with their patronizing innuendos and reports, he went back on the street and started his new sanctuary under a local bridge. There, he and others like him searched for their own semblance of reality. One of the homeless vets at a Salvation

Army meal center told him about a Macy's program that tried to help homeless vets by hiring and paying them to be Santas and Snowmen for their stores over the holidays.

Bill, figuring he had nothing to lose, went the next day and applied. The person taking the application asked him if he was a Vietnam vet. He hesitantly said he was. Told to put down his years of service and any medals, ribbons or commendations, he complied. The Silver Star and Bronze Star with clusters and five purple hearts secured him a position.

Fearing his emotional state, the Santa job was out of the question. However, as a high school student, he had been a mime for many school functions. A snowman definitely fit his ability and aptitude.

Snowmen were assigned to stand at each corner of Macy's block. Bill lucked out and was given the one spot near the front entrance to the store.

He was an instant hit his first year—his mime technique so convincing that many people were startled when he moved. Macy's even allowed Bill to take the costume home and use it for other activities, as long as he attributed Macy's with the costume and idea.

Word of Bill's remarkable snowman act caught on in a big way, and he was in demand at parties. Many well-to-do parents hired him and had their yards sprayed with man-made snow, even that next summer.

After a resounding performance in the local Eddie Bauer's, the store gave him an extra bonus: a watertight canvas bag—the kind water-rafters use—to protect the costume.

The first snow of Bill's second season, in front of Macy's, was about to change his life forever. Jerry Howard, ten, and his father, Ron, had been shopping, and walked out the front door with bundles of presents for Jerry's sister and mother. They were both talking and laughing as they paused by the snowman.

A right arm slowly moved to his mouth and removed the corncob pipe. The black-smudged eyes looked down at Jerry and said, "Merry Christmas. You dropped a present."

Jerry jumped toward his father; his dad jumped back—four eyes bugged wide.

"I didn't mean to startle you both," Snowman said. "Just thought you'd want to know about the present."

"You're good," Ron said. "Really good. Have you been doing this a long time?"

"This is my second year. I'm very happy being a snowman. It's the best job I've had lately."

"We've got to go. But keep up the good work. Maybe we'll see you around . . . oh, yes, thanks for telling Jerry about the present."

When they got home, Jerry told the story to the rest of the family. Ron kept talking about how great the snowman had been. After dinner, while reading the paper, he noticed an article about the Macy's program and how it benefited vets in the Cleveland area. His mind flashed on the previous encounter.

Ron and Jerry went back to Macy's the following weekend specifically to see the snowman, but he wasn't in his normal spot. Entering the store, Ron asked the kiosk information lady, "Have you seen Snowman? He's usually out front."

"He's over at the veteran's hospital entertaining. Our store manager thought it was a great idea when Bill suggested performing there. He's been working there one day a week for the last three months, and we've received positive feedback from the vets. They like to see a down-and-out vet make it."

Has he got a name besides Snowman?"

"Bill Mason is his real name, but he responds to Mr. Snowman. Some people prefer anonymity."

"Here's my card. Would you see that he gets it?"

"Sure . . . ah, Mr. Howard. And why do you want to talk to him? We want to protect Bill. He's had a hard life since coming home from Vietnam."

"I don't know his background, but I can guarantee you I would never hurt him. I know people, including myself, who might hire him to work parties. He has a special gift."

It was a month or more before Bill called Ron and came to the house. "I was given your card a while back," Bill said. "Been too busy to get with you—the season and all."

"I've got a birthday party for Jerry coming up in three weeks, and wanted to know if you'd be interested in working it? We've hired a Santa and sleigh and the whole neighborhood's invited."

"Let me check my schedule and get back to you. I know the store has some events they want me to work. Can you give me a couple of days?"

"No problem," Ron said.

The next afternoon Bill called Ron and told him he was free of commitments in two weeks, and would be happy to work the party. "I've also worked up a Christmas song routine that makes the outfit sound like it has a music machine inside."

The day of the party Ron picked Bill up in the morning and took him to their large garage so no one would see the arrival. He relaxed in the adjoining furnished loft until time to don his costume and take his place.

Last nights snow, like refined cotton, puffed and drifted in a game of scurry with the breeze. Bill placed himself in a covered gazebo and had brushed his trailing steps away with a broom.

Able to view the fun activities brought meaning as well as sadness back to Bill. He couldn't help but reflect on how his wife and children would have enjoyed a party like this.

The party wound down and everyone gathered around the gazebo for ice cream and cake. Jerry and his mother cut the cake and had each child come inside the gazebo to be served the dessert. When each child held out their hand and received a piece, the Snowman whispered, "Yum."

Some kids were so startled they dropped the cake. The first two children kept trying to tell the crowd that the snowman talked, but no one believed them, because there was only music coming from the costume.

When they all had received dessert, Snowman turned his head and started to sing. Some children ran, while others started laughing and crowded closer.

As the party wound down, Jerry and Ron were talking to the snowman when they noticed a black tear trickling from a coal-etched eye.

"Why are you sad, Snowman?" Jerry asked.

"Your party reminded me of my children and family at better times in my life. "I shouldn't be telling you this. You both are having a fun time. I really enjoy surprising people," he said, tipped his hat and started to walk to the loft to change.

"Hold on. I can appreciate that," Ron said. "You do appear to really enjoy your work. I did a little digging about you." He could see the startled concern clouding Bill's eyes. "Not in a bad way, Bill. I just wanted to know what you'd done before the military and during the conflict."

"Jack-of-all-trades before. Vietnam—tunnel rat, four tours."

"I'm a mine engineer and a consultant. I've got mines all over the country that I inspect for companies that hire me. I could sure use a tunnel rat that was trained in mine safety-violation detection."

"I don't think I ever want to be a tunnel rat again."

"Not even to save lives. Mining's dangerous. Add that to the fact that companies have owners, supervisors, and managers who want to make a name for themselves and are willing to skimp on safety. You earned medals for bravery and saving American lives with your military services. All I'm asking is if you want to be well paid and save more American lives.

"You can move from under the bridge to a nice place. I'd help you get established and train you. You'd work undercover. It's not without some danger if the wrong people find out what you're doing."

"When do you have to have an answer?" Bill asked.

"I'm due at the next mine in three weeks. It'll take two weeks to train you."

"I'll give you an answer in two days."

The following day Bill wandered the homeless camps around the city, when he stumbled on a sixteen-year-old street performer, doing robotics, mime impressions, and break dancing. After the performance, he approached the boy.

"Hey, Spinner. You are too cool, man."

"Well, if it ain't Snowman."

"Making any bread?"

"Comme ci, comme ca. You do the best you can in these times. Not a lot throwin' twenties anymore."

"How'd you like to move up to the big time? Steady work."

"Doin' what?"

How'd you like to be, Snowman? You could still keep part of your routine. I can get you into Macy's."

"Where you goin'?"

"I've been offered a job that moves around a lot . . . wouldn't have time. Need to know by tomorrow."

"Like, when do I start, dude."

"Meet me tomorrow morning at Macy's, ten sharp. I'll take you to the boss myself."

The Macy's manager was sorry to see Bill go, but proud they had helped him on his way to recovery, and trusted his recommendation of Spinner. Bill turned his bag and costume over to Spinner and stayed for one trial performance. He saw himself for the first time outside the costume when Spinner did his mime routine.

The following day he called Ron and accepted the job. He'd packed his belongings, put cheer in his pocket, joy on his shoulder, waved goodbye to his canvas sanctuary, and trudged toward his future.

* * * *

Three weeks later, he entered the Miracle mine bucket in West Virginia as a redneck, wearing the red bandana that all new miners in that part of the country had to wear. As the bucket started to descend, his mind drifted to another time, another place: his first rat hole.

The bucket jerked to a stop. Bill peered at the cavern, then stepped into his nether world and smiled. *The fox is in the foxhole.*

Madeline's Gift

Madeline Louise Cisco approached her first birthday, Christmas day 2030, and had already met the most difficult challenge of her young life: staying alive. Born with two damaged valves in her heart and only one lung; she'd needed a miracle.

Warm and cuddly at birth with black spiked-hair, come-hither green eyes like her father, a light island tan like her mother, she never received that first warm embrace mother and child want and need to bond. She'd been taken from the womb to NICU, isolated for one month and, since she lived, released to caretakers. There'd only been one discarded child's home in Portland, Oregon that could handle a baby like Madeline.

Nancy and Terry Cisco had waited to have children while they established themselves in the workplace. She was the media director for Channel 46, Portland, Oregon. Forty-two years old, her doctor had warned her there was a strong possibility something could go wrong—her brother, Don, a late-in-life baby, had been born with Down syndrome. She loved her brother and admired her mother for not resorting to abortion.

She and Terry had always had a better than average life, not complete, but a good life. They never had any real-world problems: the plans for the house, furniture, and their future, had always been made together.

Terry had been a teacher and administrator for twenty-nine years and had success at every position. He'd moved from one local school district to another in order to position himself for his last working goal: District Superintendent. With a severe economic depression (surpassing the Great Depression of the 1930's) settling in for the long haul, the superintendent's job wasn't going to happen, but how to tell Nancy. Realistically, he could be cut for a less expensive teacher with fewer benefits and pay, or forced to retire early. Rumors were flying that the retirement board had made more than a few bad investments, but that didn't stop anyone with over twenty-five years tenure from taking a nickel-handshake—golden parachutes/handshakes had not been around since 2008. The decision was difficult but he knew what had to be done. He and Nancy had to come first for once.

He chose that next Saturday for a heart-to-heart talk with her. His decision couldn't be made lightly; there'd have to be sacrifices on both sides. Nancy, on the other hand, would have to hire an assistant to help at the station as she neared maternity leave.

After their discussion she pondered and cried the rest of the day. Would it be worth giving up everything she had worked for? She'd always dreamed of having children with Terry and decided Sunday to talk to her pastor, mother, father, and sister. They all said the same thing: " . . . your decision, Nancy".

The decision made, the unthinkable happened: during the second trimester checkup the ultrasound identified major heart and lung problems. Decisions had to be made and made fast.

"I told you before, Terry, because of my brother, Don, I don't believe in abortion. Yet, I don't know that we're ready to take on a severely handicapped child. I realize it's our only chance for children."

"I think we should talk it over with the rest of your family and not make a hasty decision. Your mom wasn't going to let anything stop her from having Don. You know how close the two of you are, although he's ten years younger."

"It's just that I'm scared. I don't know that we're totally committed at our age. The cost alone! Can you imagine the cost? If this depression gets worse, we may both be out of work, and probably little if any medical insurance. How would we save her then?"

"I still think we should talk it over with your family. Your dad has always helped us in a pinch. You know your parents want a grandchild. Let's not rush into a decision we'll regret later."

They both agreed to talk to her parents. Terry had no immediate family to lean on for support. His folks had been killed in a car wreck seven days after he and Nancy married. His only other relative, a brother, Luke, had been killed, ten years prior, in the Iran war. Terry had tried to move on, but the events had affected his honeymoon, marriage, and contributed to a minor drinking problem that up until now had not gotten out of hand. This could be his last tragedy-straw.

The following weekend, the family meeting started well. But when Nancy's dad told her he couldn't help pay for operations and support she and Terry if they lost their jobs, she blurted out, "That makes the decision easier. I received notice three days ago; they're closing the station and everyone will get pink slips—no transfers."

Terry was startled and said as much. "Why didn't you tell me before today. I was holding off until after the meeting today with your family to tell you: I put in for early retirement. However, when I found out that our retirement fund lost over forty percent of its worth, I tried to rescind my letter—the district refused."

"I don't know what to tell you," her dad said. "I've got to evaluate what your mom and I have left to live on if this depression lasts. My retirement board is talking about cutting benefits and pay, and your mother's Social Security and Medicare benefits may not last."

Terry's view wavered through the bottom of a wine bottle after that meeting. No motivation, no desire to accomplish anything—his whiskers, the yard and life in general all needed trimming.

The beautiful home, once the envy of neighbors, groaned with disapproval. Light textured walls struggled to hold out the gloom of each passing day. Flower stems, straining their necks for one last drop of salvation, one last bloom, received only a dry thud:

another wine bottle tossed from the bedroom deck kicked-up tired dust, ughed of emptiness, then clinked to a stop against Golden Pond Cabernet.

The brown-stained sun shaded its eye when Nancy waddled onto the deck. "Can't you help until I give birth? I know we're almost out of savings, and you've mortgaged everything to the hilt, but please! I'm begging you," she cried. "This is hard enough without your drinking. Don't you ever think about anyone else anymore? I'm barely hanging in there. It's for the baby. My health is all she'll have to possibly survive. I feel so alone, and my mind is starting to slip like Grandma Margaret, Mom's mom. Grandma was only forty-one when her dementia started. I don't remember things like I used to. I need you."

When she turned to go back into the house, he staggered to his feet and followed her to the unmade bed with the filthy sheets. After she curled into a fetal position, he stood, silent, looking down on someone he knew he was supposed to love and care for. It wasn't her Terry in this nebulous void of time and space, but another: A lost and lonely creature who could only question his own worth to live, much less she and the baby.

Tugged by an undercurrent of guilt, he sank into the bed. Flailed momentarily at the mental waves engulfing him, sank deeper. Swept to the bottom he rolled onto his left side, reached out to save her and drifted away.

A two-week notice to quit the property had been posted on their front door during the night. Decision time was at hand.

Her father had helped them file personal bankruptcy to save some items; the rest would have to go. Scalpers, hawkers, and early bird scavengers swooped in at the yard sale. Again her father helped hold the prices to realistic sums—no unknown gems were in the fish bowl or hidden in the garage or attic.

Saved items went into storage in her dad's garage. Not much

to really speak of, maybe enough for a small flat, if they ever got back on their feet.

With over thirty-five percent of the workforce in the country out of work, and no prospects with the depression, they needed to talk Kroger out of two shopping carts—most people stole them. The store manager had never had anyone ask before. He not only gave them the cart but, contributed can goods and other non-perishable food items, including a manual can opener, to start them on their way.

Reality hit home when they wandered through the city park, after her release from the hospital, lost eyes watched from hundreds of temporary dwellings as the newbies pushed their carts toward the office/bathhouse that the police ran—a roster maintained of all parties and their property for future crime reports. Shelter under a hanging eve cost them ten percent of all their can-goods. The next day they struck out on their own and located a temporary future home on one of Terry's old school grounds: a 4H/FFA building that wasn't used anymore because of budget cuts. It was only two miles from her parents home, where they could go on Sundays and be guaranteed a hot meal and shower.

* * * *

Years yearned to be free of burdens. Time and memories distanced themselves. They still had a meager existence and were down to one filled Kroger shopping cart, two bedrolls, and a four-person tent her father gave them they called home.

Every Christmas Eve had been the same since living on the street. Those that could, sang, while others scrounged for some tangible insignificant gift to exchange, even discarded fruit. This year was different—more children than ever before—it made her mind twinge. How long had it been? Ten, or was it twelve years tonight she went to the hospital? Madeline? Was that her name? Had she been born? I think so. Midnight, wasn't it? There, then gone forever like part of her memory? The baby's survival had been the only thing on Nancy's mind.

The bonfire celebration was large this year. The city and shelter groups had donated extra firewood, instead of old tires for the homeless who couldn't get into shelters and remained on the street.

Nearing midnight, the unfortunates, as they were called, gathered around the fire beckoning the no-name children to stand in front of them. Carols broke out as many tried to remember the words and join in—the children's angelic voices lifting everyone's spirits.

The adults made sure all the children had something to eat and a place to sleep for the night, as the last song echoed from hovels amidst puffy flakes. Church bells tolled the hour of rebirth.

Nancy and Terry had taken a small girl home with them and shared their bedrolls. This year was the first time they'd even thought of sharing what little they had with anyone.

A fresh blanket of white hope covered the canvas igloos, and the occupants—one by one—climbed forth and prepared for the breakfast hunt.

Nancy woke, rubbed her red-rimmed, brown eyes and felt around—no little girl, no Terry. Next to where her head had rested was an old looking coin on the sack pillow the little girl had used.

What a strange thing to leave. Can't do much with a penny.

However, when she picked up the coin and put on her glasses to see through the light stain on the metal, eyes tried to register a memory—the date, 1793, and the word 'liherty', instead of 'liberty'. She gasped and yelled, "Terry where are you? Come quick."

"Yes!" Someone yelled from outside. "Right there."

"The little girl. Where's the little girl?"

"She's out here by the fire. We were going to go look for a Christmas breakfast for all three of us. She knows where they throw away day-old sweet rolls, and on Christmas day they leave two dozen coffee cakes next to the dumpster for anyone passing by. If you find the coffee cake, there's a certificate for a free cup of coffee. We were . . . " He paused and stuck his head in.

"Forget the cake," she whispered. "Do you know what this is?" Her fist uncurled one finger at a time until the coin could be seen in the palm of her hand.

"It's a penny, silly."

"No! There was something about a special set of pennies. I...I think I remember my father had a coin collection before the depression. There was something about a fifth and last penny cast in error."

"So? He had had a collection . . . some old coins and pretty gold ones. Big deal. He never gave any of them to us. It was your sister that got the collection on her wedding day. What are you trying to say?"

"I . . . I remember now. He told me when I got married that he had a very special gift for his first grandchild. He wanted grandchildren in the worst way. My sister had her profession and had said she would never have children. I . . . Oh! God! I was selfish and wanted a profession first, until we tried to have children. It's my fault, all my fault. Where's that girl? Who is she?"

She and Terry went outside, but the girl was gone. Nancy began to cry. Terry tried to hold her but she shook her head, pushed away and wandered from hovel to hovel asking about the little girl.

An hour later, the girl was back with coffee and coffee cake for the three of them.

Terry took the items from her, and Nancy held the girl gently by the shoulders. "Wha . . . what's your name? When were you born?"

"What's the matter? Did I do something wrong?"

"No. You didn't do anything wrong. I thought you might be someone I knew once."

"My name's Madeline Albright. The people at the home told me I was born on Christmas day, and they gave me my name because I was always cheery and tried to help others. They told me that my parents gave me away because they didn't have the money for major operations. No one wanted an unhealthy child. Later, an unknown person contacted the home and paid for part of my operations. The doctors at St. Agnes hospital donated the rest. Lately, the economic depression caused the home to run low on money and they asked us older kids if we would volunteer to leave. I thought I could make it on my own and give the younger kids a place to stay. Fourteen of us left to live on the streets."

"Where'd you get that coin?"

"Just before I left the orphanage, a package came for me. The coin and a note were inside. The note said, 'Share this coin only with those who demonstrate unconditional love,' signed, 'Your Benefactor'. My first night on the streets, you shared all you had with me and made me feel very special."

Nancy hugged Madeline, icy tears held to her cheeks.

Terry's wino smile widened; baggy, heavy-wool arms embraced them both. "Now I've got two best reasons in the world to quit drinking," he said, warming all three, body and soul.

"Welcome home, Madeline."

The Christmas Bike

CJ DuBoix was twelve years old, in 1932, and lived in the country near England, Arkansas. Since turning eleven, he'd dreamed of only two things he wanted more than anything else in life and found one under the tree on Christmas morning: A bike his father had built from scrap parts.

Taking it outside, his dad reminded him the chain guard was not complete. CJ hurriedly rolled up his right pant leg.

The ebony paint job, coupled with chrome rims and spokes, glistened in the sun. The custom-made handlebars curled toward the seat like horns on a Texas steer. A rearview mirror adorned the left handlebar, and a squirrel's tail was tied to the rear fender for good luck. The front fork and seat had coil springs to produce a secure, smooth ride. However, his father had warned, if a hole or large object was impacted CJ would be jolted into a physics lesson: action, reaction. Fortunately, he had yet to make that encounter, but had been witness to many at his school—boys showing off. *Not a pretty sight.*

A running start, he jumped on the seat. The front wheel skittered on some road gravel, then the whole bike wobbled to the shoulder—a smoother ride.

Be careful.

The red and black plastic handgrip streamers snapped in the breeze the faster he pedaled.

The neighbor girl, Emma Kate O'Fallon—whom CJ had a crush on—would definitely want to ride it, he thought, and sped the mile between their houses to show off the bike. He stopped on the road near her home and called.

The southern tomboy cutie with freckles and pigtails burst out the door, hollered, "I'll be right back," and ran to him.

"Can I ride it?" she asked, admiring the new bike and batting her long lashes, green-eyes sparkling in the sunshine. "I've never had a bike."

"No. I just got it for Christmas; it's not even broken in."

"Can I ride it after you break it in?"

"I'll see."

"How long will it take to break it in?"

"At least six months to a year."

"Why?"

"Why what?"

"Why will it take that long?"

"Because."

"Because why?"

"You're driving me nuts with your questions. Why don't you stop?"

"I asked you first."

"You asked me what, first?"

"Why?"

"No wonder my dad tells my mom, 'a man can never understand a woman', or in your case—a girl."

"That's what my mom says about men . . . and boys like you."

"Well . . . I've gotta go. Almost time for lunch."

Emma Kate gave him a shy smile and said, "I could give you a kiss for a ride."

CJ's face blanched as he jumped on the bike and raced away.

That evening, after supper, he said, "Daddy. Can I ask you a question?"

"What is it, son?"

"Well . . . you know Emma Kate. She asked to ride my bike, but I said not until it's broken in."

"It's your bike, son. You have to be responsible for it. I'll leave it up to you when you want to let others ride."

"There's just one catch. She wants to give me a kiss for a ride."

He hid a concerned smile behind the newspaper he was reading and said, "That's a hard decision to make. I'd probably want to sleep on it."

"Thanks, Daddy," he said, bounding from the room. Later, from his bedroom window, he watched a light snow sprinkle the ground and pondered the decision.

CJ woke, his mind at ease, dressed and rode off down the road, mud spattering his clothes and shoes. Sunrise had melted the night's white remnants.

Around nine, Emma Kate came up the road. She had on brand new bib-overalls, with extra-long legs—room to grow.

"What're ya doing this morning?" she asked, angling her come-hither smile. "Did ya think about what I said yesterday?"

"Yes. I did. I even talked to my dad. He said it was up to me."

"Well. Can I?"

"Ok. But I get my kiss first."

"Lean over the bike," she said, looked around, and gave a light peck on his cheek. "Now it's my turn."

"That wasn't a kiss," he protested. "All I felt was your wet nose. Not fair. No kiss, no ride," he said, and locked a two-handed grip on the handlebars.

"Oh, all right. Turn your cheek and lean over here."

When she went to kiss his cheek, he turned his head and their lips met. Her eyes widened and darted. "My . . . my turn, now."

"Ok. But stay on this road, be careful of the gravel, and don't go too far," he said, and watched her start the ride.

She hadn't gone more than ten yards, when he knew by her rapid pedaling she was headed for thrill hill and ran after her.

He reached the top of the hill, gasping for breath, and saw her standing with what remained of his bike: handlebars twisted, seat askew, paint scratched, and no squirrel tail. The rearview mirror, spokes and chrome rims survived—*thank you bike gods*.

Emma Kate started hopping, her right pant leg caught in the chain and sprocket.

On the verge of crying, he ran down the hill yelling, "What did you do to my new bike?"

"Your bike," she whined. "My mom's going to kill me! These overalls are brand new, and now look at them, torn and greasy. They're my one and only Christmas present."

"Well, this is my first bike!"

A familiar voice yelled for her. She drew in a quick breath and whispered, "Oh, no! That's, Momma."

"I'll say I was giving you a ride and your pants got caught and tipped us over." He helped her rotate the sprocket releasing the pant leg from the chain.

"Thanks for the ride," she said, then ran up the hill yodeling, "I'm coming."

CJ resolutely pushed the wounded bike home.

His father watched him approach, "What happened to the bike?"

"I tipped over on thrill hill."

"Let's go to the shed and see if we can fix it."

Setting the bike on a handmade stand in the workshop and

retrieving his tools, he peered through the bike frame and asked, "Was it worth it?"

"All I can say, Daddy," face beaming, "this has been the best Christmas of my life."

"I know, son. that's why I asked. I love you and don't want anything to happen to you. You do realize Emma Kate is white?"

About the Author

Bud Hanks started writing short stories and poetry thirty years ago for family and contests. The writings started from snippets of situations and people's conversations along life's way.

Retired law enforcement officer and teacher, he moved to Fayetteville, Arkansas with his wife and started writing at the Northwest Arkansas Writer's Workshop. He belongs to Ozark Writer's League and Ozark Creative Writers, where he's won numerous awards.

www.ingramcontent.com/pod-product-compliance
Lightning Source LLC
Chambersburg PA
CBHW032108170626
46808CB00008B/2980

* 9 7 8 0 9 9 1 2 6 4 1 9 3 *